MW01282108

LORGAR

BEARER OF THE WORD

THE HORUS HERESY®

The Primarchs

LORGAR: BEARER OF THE WORD
Gav Thorpe

PERTURABO: THE HAMMER OF OLYMPIA
Guy Haley

MAGNUS THE RED: MASTER OF PROSPERO
Graham McNeill

LEMAN RUSS: THE GREAT WOLF
Chris Wraight

ROBOUTE GUILLIMAN: LORD OF ULTRAMAR
David Annandale

More Word Bearers from Black Library

THE FIRST HERETIC
Aaron Dembski-Bowden

BETRAYER
Aaron Dembski-Bowden

THE UNBURDENED
David Annandale

AURELIAN
Aaron Dembski-Bowden

THE PURGE
Anthony Reynolds

WORD BEARERS: THE OMNIBUS
Anthony Reynolds
(Contains the novels *Dark Apostle, Dark Disciple* and *Dark Creed*)

CHILDREN OF SICARIUS
Anthony Reynolds (audio drama)

The Horus Heresy®

PRIMARCHS

GAV THORPE

LORGAR

BEARER OF THE WORD

This book would not have been possible without First Chaplain Ant Reynolds and Keeper of the Faith Kor Ph-Aaron.

A BLACK LIBRARY PUBLICATION

First published in 2017.
This edition published in Great Britain in 2017 by
Black Library,
Games Workshop Ltd.,
Willow Road,
Nottingham, NG7 2WS, UK.

10 9 8 7 6 5 4 3 2 1

Produced by Games Workshop in Nottingham.
Cover illustration by Mikhail Savier.

A CIP record for this book is available from the British Library.

ISBN 13: 978 1 78496 608 9

Printed and bound in China

THE HORUS HERESY®

It is a time of legend.

Mighty heroes battle for the right to rule the galaxy. The vast armies of the Emperor of Mankind conquer the stars in a Great Crusade – the myriad alien races are to be smashed by his elite warriors and wiped from the face of history.

The dawn of a new age of supremacy for humanity beckons. Gleaming citadels of marble and gold celebrate the many victories of the Emperor, as system after system is brought back under his control. Triumphs are raised on a million worlds to record the epic deeds of his most powerful champions.

First and foremost amongst these are the primarchs, superhuman beings who have led the Space Marine Legions in campaign after campaign. They are unstoppable and magnificent, the pinnacle of the Emperor's genetic experimentation, while the Space Marines themselves are the mightiest human warriors the galaxy has ever known, each capable of besting a hundred normal men or more in combat.

Many are the tales told of these legendary beings. From the halls of the Imperial Palace on Terra to the outermost reaches of Ultima Segmentum, their deeds are known to be shaping the very future of the galaxy. But can such souls remain free of doubt and corruption forever? Or will the temptation of greater power prove too much for even the most loyal sons of the Emperor?

The seeds of heresy have already been sown, and the start of the greatest war in the history of mankind is but a few years away...

THE EMBERS

959.M30

Forty-Seven Nine (formerly Hierapolis)

The Tower of Infinite Lords was less impressive than its name suggested. Three storeys high, hexagonal, a pilaster of white gold rising from the peak of its roof, it was in fact smaller than any one of the weapons turrets on the *Fidelitas Lex*. But the structure exerted a dominance over Forty-Seven Nine that more than justified its title.

'I was expecting something bigger,' said Captain Jarulek. Like his skin beneath, Jarulek's grey armour was covered in a continuous tracery of cuneiform – neatly inscribed passages from the *Book of Lorgar* in the tongue of Colchis, a sign of its wearer's devotion.

At his back stood forty Word Bearers, their slab-grey armour anointed with blessed oils that glistened on squad markings and the rune of the Perpetual Spiral Chapter. With them came Chaplain Melchiades, though Kor Phaeron had known him better as Dar Voldak back on Colchis.

The First Captain, the Keeper of Faith, favoured of the Urizen, had taken personal command of the last assault on the bastion of the church that called itself the Silvered Cup. Across Hierapolis the cult's shrines and followers had burned. The last were to be slain that day by order of Lorgar Aurelian. With Kor Phaeron were ten Space Marines of the Ashen Circle, warriors sworn to the destruction of all false idols and heresies.

'It is but a capstone, I believe,' said Kor Phaeron. 'If the confessions extracted from the non-compliant are to be trusted, the tower sits atop a necropolis that stretches beneath most of this city.'

He cast an arm to encompass the ruins that surrounded them, buildings levelled by orbital and Whirlwind missile bombardment the previous day. Amidst all of the destruction, and despite the ferocity of the attack, the tower still stood. The official Legion reports put this endurance down to a concealed energy field of some kind. Kor Phaeron suspected that a more otherworldly force was at play, hence his decision to intervene directly in its razing, legitimising the presence of his own men in the guise of the Ashen Circle – men who knew the Truth could not be buried nor burned.

'It doesn't even have guns,' scoffed one of Jarulek's subordinates, a sergeant named Bel Ashared. Kor Phaeron was of a mind to recommend the squad leader to Erebus for promotion to the ranks of the Legion's Chaplains and this expedition was, though Bel Ashared did not know it, a test of temperament – and loyalties.

'Then you will not shirk from being the first through the gates,' replied Kor Phaeron, pointing his chainblade towards the tower's ornate entrance.

'The Emperor wills it, it shall be done.' Bel Ashared raised his bolter in acceptance of the challenge and then signalled for his squad to make ready for the attack.

Melchiades stepped forwards, a grim figure in black, a tabard of grey over his armour reminiscent of the Covenant priests of their home world – a sign that he had been raised from infancy in the embrace of the holy church. Like Kor Phaeron himself, though the Keeper of Faith needed no such decoration for others to know his storied history.

'Dwellers within,' the Chaplain declared, his voice amplified to a roar by his armour's address system, ringing back from the stone walls. 'You have been found guilty of non-compliance with the desires of the Emperor of Mankind, refusing the benefits of Enlightenment and denying the Imperial Truth. In persisting with your worship of false gods you directly defy the mandates of Terra. Furthermore, in refusing to acknowledge the falsity of your worship you commit the wilful and persistent adherence to an error in matters of faith.

'There is but one Lore and Law, and it is from Him of Terra that it springs. Font of Truth, the Emperor has claimed this world for the benefit of all humankind. You refused to set aside your selfish vanity and are therefore guilty also of treason against humanity. No clemency will be offered, no mercy shown. Your lives are forfeit and your estates shall become one with the great Imperium of Mankind.'

Such formalities observed, Jarulek signalled his warriors to advance, the squad of Bel Ashared at the spearhead of the attack. Kor Phaeron and his followers from the Ashen Circle followed close behind on foot, their hand flamers and barb-toothed axe rakes in hand, the speedy advance offered by their jump packs not required on this occasion.

Bel Ashared himself reached the silver portal first, and placed a trio of melta bombs upon its surface before withdrawing. Their detonation turned the gates to charred splinters and molten metal, ripping a hole through the thick barrier to expose the broken bars and locks within. Wrenching open the doors, the Word Bearers stormed the threshold, bolters spitting at some enemy as yet out of sight of Kor Phaeron. Sparks of las-fire flashed past the Space Marines as they stormed the breach, flicking ineffectually from their war-plate.

Entering in the wake of the assault, Kor Phaeron and his companions found themselves in a small foyer, a circular shrine ahead, the altar already toppled and broken by Jarulek's warriors. The plastered walls were painted with elaborate murals that reminded Kor Phaeron of illustrations from the oldest holy books of Colchis – depictions of the Empyrean he had studied for long years before the arrival of the Emperor and the XVII Legion. The scars of laser and bolt marked the swirling designs, among spatters of dribbling blood. Bodies torn apart by bolt detonations filled the doorways and littered the white slabs underfoot, swathed in silken vestments of the Silvered Cup faithful, their blood seeping along the cracks between the tiles. Nothing else was alive.

There was another door at the opposite side of the chapel, of plain white-painted wood. A squad of Jarulek's men stood ready to open it.

'Wait!' Kor Phaeron commanded, striding quickly across the shrine-room. 'An inner sanctum, I expect. We shall deal with the blasphemies within. Jarulek, search for routes into the catacombs – there is no telling how many of these vermin might flee through the tunnels. Coordinate with your squads scouring the city on the surface so that none escape.'

The captain hesitated for a moment, and then looked at the Ashen Circle gathering around Kor Phaeron. He raised his blade across his eye-lenses in salute and then turned away, issuing orders to his warriors.

'Dathor, break the door,' Kor Phaeron said, stepping aside for the Ashen Circle warrior to approach.

The chainblade of Dathor's axe rake snarled into life, teeth becoming a blur at its tip. With three swings he hewed at the portal, the third bedding the blade deep into the timbers, allowing him to rip the splintering fragments from the frame.

Kor Phaeron entered first, stepping into a short hallway, too narrow for the jump packs of the Ashen Circle.

'Ensure none follow,' he told them before advancing to the stairwell at the far end. He ascended quickly, into a chamber that ran the breadth of the tower.

Here he found statuary and more murals, and at the far end a handful of robed men with long beards hurriedly taking books and amulets out of a large chest. One of them noticed Kor Phaeron and straightened, panic on his face. He started to reach for something inside his robe.

'If that is a weapon, you all die in the next thirty seconds,' said Kor Phaeron. 'Stay your hand and you live. Which one of you is Audeaus?'

The five elders looked at each other before one of their number, even more wizened than the others, raised a timid hand.

'I am Audeaus, Overpriest of the Silvered Cup.' He puffed out his chest, affecting a semblance of disdain, though it was clear from his trembling hands that it was all bluster. 'This blasphemy shall not g–'

'Know that this day your prayers have been answered, Audeaus. I have seen the manner of Powers that you serve. A time of testing is at hand, but you must stay strong. Do you have means to escape this chamber?'

'I… Why are you doing this?'

'Does it matter?' snapped one of Audeaus' fellow elders. 'He is letting us go!'

'An ornithopter in a loft station,' another replied on behalf of their leader. He stepped towards a ladder that ran up one wall, pointing to a trapdoor above it.

'Nourish your faith, but remain hidden. Let the Truth be your strength, and whatever becomes of this world know that your faith will prevail. Your souls shall be rewarded. There will come a time when your true masters call upon your descendants.'

As a group they started towards the ladder. Kor Phaeron raised his bolt pistol and aimed at Audeaus.

'I must have proof that your sect has been destroyed. Your head will suffice. The rest of you, fly east for two kilometres and then north east out of the city. There is a gap in the augur screen. You will find refuge in the Midden Mires. Disappear.'

'I thought you said my prayers had been answered,' said the overpriest, alarmed. He tried to run for the ladder but the other priests snatched hold of his robes and forced him back towards Kor Phaeron.

'Did you not pray for the Powers to lay their gaze upon you?'

Audeaus nodded hesitantly. Those who had given him up hurried towards the escape route.

'Now you shall lay your gaze upon the Powers,' Kor Phaeron said, and pulled the trigger.

BOOK 1: REVELATION

COLCHIS

118 years ago [Terran standard]
24.5 years ago [Colchisian calendar]

Translator's Note on Time

The world of Colchis is of a magnitude larger than Holy Terra, and consequently even approximations of time by the accepted nomenclature of 'Terran standard' are unsuccessful in conveying the very different diurnal and nocturnal cycle of its inhabitants. Before we begin, the reader should familiarise themselves with the following information.

The orbit of Colchis around its star takes nearly five years – four point eight to be more precise. Therefore if a Colchisian refers to being six years old, they are in fact twenty-eight or twenty-nine Terran years old.

A Colchisian solar day, that is, one complete planetary rotation, is seven point one Terran days, or one hundred and seventy point four Terran hours. Clearly even humans, as adaptable as they are, cannot survive with a ninety-hour day/ night cycle, and so Colchisian culture developed a system for intermediary sleep and waking periods.

These periods are often referred to as 'days' in many volumes but this can be confusing and portray an erroneous image of events. In this text I have endeavoured to achieve a more literal translation of the Colchisian terminology, which is derived from the language of the ancient desert settlers.

'Day', in the following manuscript, refers to a complete orbital turn of the planet, from sunrise to sunrise.

This day is further divided into the following times of approximately twenty-four hours each (the exact length depends further upon seasons and locality, and chronometry on Colchis is a dedicated and difficult scientific discipline in its own right):

Dawnaway
Mornday
Long Noon
Post-noon
Duskeve
Coldfall
High Night

These sub-days are then broken down into three further periods, two of wakefulness and one of sleep, approximating eight hours each. These three periods are called wake-rise, wake-main and rest-eve, with the last being the sleep period (although frequently inhabitants may sleep less than eight hours during Mornday, Long Noon and Post-noon, and slightly longer during the darkness of the remaining time).

One might therefore refer to wake-rise of Dawnaway, being sometime in the first eight hours of the first twenty-four-hour period of a new Colchisian day. Custom has it that the hottest time, wake-main of Long Noon, is also a rest period, for when the local star is at its zenith, it is exceptionally deleterious to health to be out of cover. Conversely, rest-eve of High Night is the coldest and darkest period of the Colchisian day.

As for other such timekeeping measures such as months, local year counts and so forth, I have spared the reader all but the most scant detail, for such things are exceptionally complex and not necessary for understanding this text.

1 1 1

Sands the colour of rust, ash and old sweat stretched out to the haze-blurred horizon. Even in the baking heat some life clung on – scrubs of thorny bushes and trees, cacti and brightly flowered succulents rose in the shadows of pillar-like rocks, sustained within the meandering wadi and drawing sustenance from the deep remains of lost oases. There was movement everywhere if one knew where to look. Scorpions and sun beetles skittered over the scorching sands and flies buzzed lazily from cactus to cactus. Far above, in the wisps of cloud that scudded across a pale-blue sky, immense sand vultures with four-metre wingspans circled in the cool upper airs, eyes as powerful as magnoculars scanning the ground for any morsel.

Dust devils skirted across the dunes, erasing the tracks around the camp, piling fresh drifts against the sides of thirteen large tents made of fabric striped red and blue, black and gold, grey and white. Sunshades held up on strong poles shielded against the unrelenting Long Noon blaze, keeping the worst from the backs of prized bipedal sunstrider mounts and much more heavily set sternback sled-beasts. Their short hair stained red by the dust, the animals panted in the heat despite the shade, eyes closed against the glare coming off the nearby dunes.

More huge parasols were set up on the leeward side of the camp, and beneath them clustered the Declined. Old and young, they huddled about their solar stoves cooking patties made from grey cactus flour flavoured with treasured drops of honeyspider milk. They talked quietly and nursed their canteens – perilously low now that they were two and a half days out from the last oasis – debating the best course to take at wake-rise of Duskeve, when the dropping temperatures made travel practical again.

They fingered talismans and fetishes of small bird and mammal bones, intricately carved with verses passed down from ancient generations. The eldest dozed, clasping prayer-sticks across their chests, the faint whistles and whines from the pierced bones changing as their chests rose and fell in the constant but weak breeze. Around them infants dug in the sand for wadi-nappers and desert whelks, though in their minds they imagined they were opening up one of the Lost Vaults to unearth archeotech treasures from the time of the Last Wandering. They picked over pebbles and small fossils, dividing them into piles of varying shininess, size and other criteria only small children would understand.

The older children dared each other to stand in the sun for as long as possible, timing their efforts with small sandglasses, ignoring the warnings of their parents who spoke of some uncle or aunt who had died from a skin-curdling sunrash or been consumed by swarms of tumours.

The youngest adults attended to the shrine. The centre of the camp was dominated by four large poles, each made up of separate totems carved in the many likenesses of the four Powers. Though they were Declined, forbidden entry into any of the great cities, they nevertheless paid homage to the gods of their ancestors as best they could. Offerings of small sacrifices burned in incense bowls at the base of each pole, their scented wisps drifting out across the camp, carrying the prayers of the faithful into the air. The ward-priests kept the small fires burning, moving from one to the next in constant work, wafting air, rearranging kindling, adding sprinkles of more incense where required.

Now and then one of the nomads would rouse in the stupefying heat, struck by a sudden thought or need. They would scribble their prayer on a scrap of papyrus and pass it to one of the totem-attendees. Murmured incantations would accompany the flare of burning papyrus, their meaning lost to antiquity, but their importance sustained over a hundred generations.

1 1 2

Fan Morgai, leader of the tribe, gathered his family to a brief council. He pointed to the darker shimmer on the horizon, which a stranger to the deserts might have mistaken for a mountain. The nomads knew better – the mound whose peak was just visible in the distance was no natural formation but the remains of a city of their ancestors, long dead sands claimed by the desert.

'Two more rest-eves, with good walking,' he told them, waving the fabric map that was his most prized heirloom. The symbols were all but faded from view, but he knew how to read the topography, taught by his mother and grandfather as soon as he was old enough to learn his letters.

'A prayer in a hole,' muttered Stanzia, his eldest sister. 'You think the gods will guide us to a Lost Vault?'

'No,' Fan Morgai said with a sad shake of the head. 'I think that this is the City of Mirrors. See the clouds above it. Rain, my boys and girls. Rain soon.'

'The wadi at Fushas is said to be flooded again,' said his youngest cousin, Fabri Tal. 'Only a wake-rise's walk away, no more.'

'The wrong way,' argued Kora, Fabri Tal's elder brother, who had already expressed his favour for the plan of Fan Morgai. 'And who said this? A drunken soothsayer at Maiporis? He would tell you anything for a sip of j'kahs.'

'He had one of the old books,' protested Fabri Tal, 'and he cast the bones upon its pages right in front of me, I saw. A wind symbol and the sun. Fresh beginnings, he told me.'

'And you spared him a sip of your liquor for the good news,' said Fan Morgai. He was about to continue but a shrill call drew all their attention to the shaded watchpost on stilts erected at the windward side of the camp. Others were standing, shielding their eyes against the glare.

'Go, Alannat, swap with Benjor,' Fan Morgai told his young sister, and she dashed off into the light, sweeping her headscarf about her face to shield against the sun for the moments it took her to reach the watchpost.

Benjor dropped down and ran back to the elder, his looking-tube glinting in his hand. He gestured for Fan Morgai to meet him between the two nearest tents and pointed into the wind, a little to edgewards.

'Caravan!' he blurted, thrusting the seeing device to Fan Morgai. 'Caravan!'

The tribal leader lifted the telescope to his eye. Retinal detectors clicked and whirred as they adjusted the liquid lens, bringing the horizon into sharper focus. He swept right a little, towards the far distant coast, and caught a blur of darkness against the dunes, no more than a kilometre away.

'Caravan, out here?' He looked at Stanzia and they shared a glance of concern. They both looked to the main tent that housed the chief's family.

'Say nothing to the strangers,' she told him and he agreed with a nod.

'Make ready, get your weapons,' he told the others. 'But do nothing to provoke them and let me do the talking.'

1 1 3

The largest vehicle crested a broad dune like a breaching whale, its huge flanks rearing up over the sands amid a plume of dust and smoke. A dozen small funnels trailed oily fumes from their gargoyle caps. Thick wooden tracks churned the sand as it achieved the summit, the sand plough upon its front furrowing aside dirt and grit into twin banks on either side.

Details were scant, the caravan just a vague darkness in the haze, but as the vehicle approached the other shapes around it resolved into better focus. Two-crew four-wheelers ran as outriders, their roofs and spoilers glinting with solar collecting plates, balloon tyres carrying them over the shifting desert.

With them came actual riders, mounted on sunstriders decked in faded ribbons and pennants, the streamer of a black-and-red prayer flag curling from the back of each scout. Their faces were hidden by thick scarves and glare goggles, their riding robes tattered and dirty. Their steeds had also seen better days, flanks scarred by sandstorms, hair matted, tails docked short in the style of the inner waste tribes.

Other vehicles followed, forming an entourage for the temple-rig – carts pulled by threesomes of dromedores, and sunstrider chariots, two of them, each hauling chains and weighted flags through the sand to obscure the trail left by the caravan.

The shrine wagon could now be seen more clearly, a turret above its driver's cab topped by numerous flared speakers flanking a pulpit, large reflectors casting a brightness onto the decking behind, where dozens of armed men and women waited. As the great sheet above the deck flapped and bulged in the winds, spear-tips and mauls, arrows and slingstaves glinted in occasional flashes of sunshine. Beyond the stacks of the traction engine the large wagon heaped up into a type of aft castle, upon which two spear-launchers were mounted. Here mast-like poles were joined to the exhaust piles by black and red bunting, missing in places, giving the impression of gap-toothed grins.

From the summit glinted a golden icon, of a book aflame. A symbol of allegiance and faith, a testament to one of the proselytising creeds of the old cities. The Covenant of Vharadesh.

1 1 4

The glimmer of eyepieces sparkled along the deck of the shrine wagon as the occupants turned their attention to the cluster of tents sighted in the distance. Orders were barked down the speaker tubes and the engines of the mobile chapel grumbled in response to the coaxing and curses of the crew below, hauling the unyielding vehicle onto a new course into the broad sand basin beyond the ridge.

Nairo darted between the caravan guards, scooping a ladle from his bucket to slop grease onto the exposed cogs of the running gear below the main platform. Around him the sellswords at the gunwales readied their windbows and dart guns, and loosened cudgels in their belts. A few aimed kicks at the ageing slave; others directed only curses at the man winding his way in a half-crouch between them.

He was clad only in a loincloth and headband, his whip-marked back and shoulders an exposed maze of sun-darkened skin and white scar tissue, turned leathery and cracked by years of exposure. It was, Powers be praised, a miracle Nairo had not been cursed with the tumours like so many of those he had grown up with – his advanced age was something of a talisman among the other slaves. Six Colchisian years he had survived; thirty as the adepts of Terra would later reckon such a time span.

His head was shaved bald, tattooed on the right side with a simple version of the Book of the Word, symbol of the Covenant who ostensibly owned him.

He passed fierce Cthollic mercenaries, their porcelain masks flat over their faces, decorated with cruel visages drawn from the vision-journeys of intoxicant-fuelled coming-of-age rituals. They wielded serrated spears, their jerkins adorned with discs of refractive material that gleamed white in the high sun.

Next to them the Archer Brethren – sea warriors now confined to land, their windbows resting on the side of the wagon. Fierce of expression, the men heavily bearded, the women with braids tied under their chins in imitation of the favoured facial hair.

Witchwalkers of Carthass, dispossessed by the loss of their homes, swallowed by the great earth-tumults of a year earlier. An entire great city disappeared into the sand and waters, destroyed, so it was claimed by the Covenant, for their sinful ways. This handful of survivors caked their bodies in ochre paint out of shame, its colour visible between their segmented plastrons, vambraces and greaves.

And more, from other cities and none, all of them converts. Not a single warrior was a native of the Covenant; none were born of Vharadesh, the Holy City. This simple fact made them more fervent followers, with the vigour of those whose existence now depended upon the Truth of the Word to give their lives meaning. Their adopted creed made them as zealous as their master.

Of him, of the Bearer of the Word, there was no sign, though warning had been sent to the caravan's master that a Declined camp had been sighted. Nairo cast glances at the hatchway that led to the master's chambers in the bowels of the temple-rig, but there was no movement to be seen.

1 1 5

Castora, the herald-slave, scuttled into view from the smaller entrance further aft and quickly ascended the ladder to the pulpit as the mobile shrine ground to a halt a hundred metres from the outskirts of the camp. With a scratch and amplified crackle, the address system sprang into life at her instigation.

Movement stirred in the camp as the nomads assembled at the edge of the shade cast by their covers. Nairo could see the glint of weapons – spears for the most part, nothing advanced – but the arrangement of the Declined suggested curiosity more than hostility. They could be seen talking to each other, casual in their attitude.

An automated clarion wailed several distorted notes from the prayer-hailers, cutting through the rasping wind.

'Rejoice, those who have fallen from the gaze of the Powers,' announced Castora. She spoke *waterwords,* the common language of the traders and missionaries who moved between cities. Nairo could see her face, resigned to her task though she tried her best to summon as much enthusiasm as she could for the audience. 'Celebrate the beneficence of the Powers, for this day they have guided to you the Bearer of the Word. Fear not, for he brings only counsel and wisdom for those who wish to heed it. No longer must you dwell in the wilderness of ignorance. The Bearer of the Word shall set you back upon the path to the Truth, and through his indulgences you shall know again the Will of the Powers.'

The sound of a foot upon the steps drew Nairo's eye back to the open grate. As Castora continued her speech, lauding the benefits of the Truth and the righteousness of the Bearer of the Word, the master emerged. He was young, three and a half years by the measure of Colchis' long orbit, but his brow already carried the deep furrows that would permanently twist them in later life. Gaunt he was, but not yet possessed of the lines of care and age that would mark his older years. He was garbed in dirty tatters of dark grey robes marked by sigils of the Powers and designs of the constellations of the Empyrean Above – the very same clothes that had been literally ripped from his back when he had been cast out of Vharadesh. His flesh was thin, his existence in the desolation honing his body to wiry muscle and little else. Already his skin was marked with the scars of exposure, dark from the sun and scratched from the wind-borne sands.

Castora withdrew as he reached the bottom of the pulpit ladder, slipping over the edge like a fleeing serpent to allow the master to ascend without obstruction. With characteristic energy he hauled himself up to the addressing platform while the clarions sounded their grating call again.

'Heed the Bearer of the Word,' he declared, raising his arms above his head. 'Witness the Truth from my lips and remember the name of Kor Phaeron!'

1 2 1

The leader of the Declined raised his hand, giving the caravan permission to approach. The temple-rig rolled forwards at walking pace while the other vehicles formed a boundary about it and the escorts dropped down from the fighting platform to walk alongside in a guard of honour. Two sandsleds pulled ahead, raising up great sails to create a corridor of shadow between the lowering gangplank of the mobile shrine and the perimeter of shade at the edge of the camp.

Kor Phaeron swung himself over the side onto a rope ladder and swiftly climbed down to the shaded sand, his bare feet sinking into the heated grains. He hardly felt their scorching touch through scars and calluses as thick as the bottom of a shoe – it was a joke amongst his coterie that his soles were as inured to pain as his soul. He permitted such humour to continue as long as it was not deliberately perpetrated within earshot. Mockery of the Powers and the Empyrean was a blasphemy, of course, but he also knew that soldiers had their own ways and it was better not to test their loyalty too hard with unnecessary injunctions on their behaviour.

A handful of the nomads clustered forwards, bearing cups

of water in welcome. It was a good sign, and Kor Phaeron felt his mood lighten at the prospect that his sermon might fall on willing ears for a change. Custom dictated that they host the preacher, but all too often such hospitality was short-lived, long enough only to satisfy tradition and reputation. The offering of water seemed a genuine welcome.

He suppressed a grimace as he saw some of the nomads were marked with the swirls of the sand-curse, or the scabby lesions of the celleater. Uncleanliness was rife amongst the Declined, a symptom of their irreligious ways, but he did not believe this justified denying them the Truth. What was the point in bearing the Word of the Powers to those who already heeded it? That the fools of Vharadesh had cast him out for suggesting that the Covenant should be more missionary in its outlook had only reinforced his belief that the Truth lay in the wilderness between cities.

That this was an apt metaphor for his endless quest through the desolation for pockets of wisdom was not lost on Kor Phaeron. Guided by the Powers through the arcane mysteries of Colchisian astrology, Kor Phaeron had recruited dozens to his cause in the long seasons since his exile had begun. There were ears that would heed the Word and the Truth, and while they did it was his duty to bring it to them.

'May our journey end in the waters,' the nomad leader said, inclining his head in greeting. He was a little shorter than Kor Phaeron, and maybe seven years old, though most of his face was hidden by scarf and goggles. The hand that proffered the cup of water was lined with age, the leathery skin cracked and tight over sparse flesh.

'Blessings of the Powers upon you,' Kor Phaeron replied, raising up his left hand with the middle and index finger together, drawing the Sign of the Four in the air as prescribed in the *Accounts of the Barabicus:* a circular motion starting at the top left and moving down and right, followed by an 'X' across the same. The nomad leader followed the movement of the fingers with a curious look, ignorant to its meeting but impressed by the import of the gesture and the solemnity with which it was delivered.

'I am Kor Phaeron, the Bearer of the Word.'

'I am Fan Morgai and these are my people.' He took a sip from the cup and passed it to Kor Phaeron, who allowed only enough liquid to moisten his lips.

He was eager to begin his sermon, but Fan Morgai was insistent that all the customs were followed. After they had drunk from the same water, he then insisted on introducing his family and other prominent members of the tribe, reeling off names that Kor Phaeron forgot immediately as irrelevant. If they became followers he would deign to spare more thought for them, but not before.

1 2 2

Eventually Kor Phaeron was guided to the mats closer to the heart of the camp, though not those directly next to the central tent as he might have expected. Rather than dwell on this strange departure from nomad tradition, he eagerly launched into his sermon, gesturing strongly to emphasise his points, dark eyes moving from one listener to the next in smooth transitions as he had been taught in the chambers of the Orastry in Vharadesh.

The heat of his passion consumed him, fuelling his words as he strayed from his practised lines to remark upon the journeys of Epixas of Eurgemez and her death at the hands of the Unbelievers of that city when she returned with the Truth. He could see understanding in the faces of his audience as they shared the pains of Epixas' tribulations and rejection, as they had been rejected by those who claimed themselves faithful.

'In each of us has been set a purpose,' he told them, glorying in the opportunity to unburden his mind of their heavy thoughts. 'The Powers look upon our works and are disdainful, for there is nothing beneath the Empyrean we can create that is not but a pale mirror to the glories of the Upper Spheres.'

The spirit of the Powers was upon him, a fire in his gut as their words passed from his lips. Theirs was the Will, his was the Word that carried it. He laid a hand upon the scarf-clad head of Fan Morgai, feeling a paternal regard for these dispossessed though most were his senior by a half-year and some much more. The Powers had ushered them into his care and he would not abdicate his responsibility to introduce them to the Truth.

'I shall not shun you as others have, for the Powers care not for our mortal hierarchies, only our dedication. It matters not that you dwell in the wild places, cast from civilisation into the desert like animals, for we are all nothing but tenants on the lands of the Powers.

'Who more than you know the meaning of sacrifice? What priest or priestess in the towers of Ghuras or Vharadesh can say they know the desires of the Powers more than those forced to suffer each day beneath their burning scrutiny?' He waved a hand towards the great orb beyond the parasol-sails. 'Make no mistake that what the sun is to the day, so the Powers are to life. They are the light that sustains it, the fire that will consume it. As the sun is relentless upon our backs, so we must be relentless in our service.'

The Declined were held rapt by these words, so different from the dry testaments of other missionaries who had sought faith for their cause. Here was one who spoke in ways that matched their experiences, who knew something of their miserable lives.

More than half the adults of the camp had gathered to listen to his sermon, and as many children as could muster a few moments of attention.

Kor Phaeron caught himself upon the crest of pride, about to plunge into the self-congratulatory trough beyond. It was not to him that they pledged their attention but to the Truth. He reminded himself he was but a vessel for the Powers, an instrument of the Will and nothing more. His was not the credit, only the sacrifice. Such was the position to which he had been appointed.

1 2 3

Kor Phaeron, possessed by the energy of the Powers, started to pace as he spoke, moving along the row of cross-legged nomads at the front of the crowd. He directed his words to those at the back, encouraging them to hearken to his message so that they might know the Truth.

'Unto us will be delivered the Word, and with it shall we know the Will of the Powers,' he told them. He clenched a fist to his sun-scarred chest. 'Into me has been passed this knowledge. I pass it to you, for the Powers have spoken and declared that the message must be heard. A time of testing will come, when the Powers turn their immortal gaze upon Colchis and judge the worthy from the unworthy. None can raise up the defence of "but I did not know" for the Powers have gifted us all with the means to know the Truth.'

He waved a hand towards the slaves bearing his accoutrements behind him – many sacred books, a sceptre with a fist-shaped head and other relics that he had come upon in his searching across the wastes. At the gesture the slaves knelt and proffered up their burdens.

'I have read the wisdom in these ancient pages,' – a half-truth, for he understood the language in only six books from his library – 'and in them I have discovered the Word. And the Word sayeth that we shall serve the Powers to the exclusion of ought else. Slaves shall provide the food, for free men and women must bear the burden of worship, bending all effort to the praises of the Powers that created and sustained us.

'Each of you is a chosen one.' He pointed at the crowd with a skinny finger. Some smiled, others flinched. He noticed Fan Morgai and a few others glance away. Kor Phaeron pondered this as he continued, 'Each has their place in the machine of the universe, whether to be the cog or the cable, the switch or the fulcrum. The texts tell us that one will come, raised above the others in the eyes of the Powers, to bring sight to the blind, hearing to the deaf, the Word to the mute.'

Again the sharp eyes of the preacher caught a small flutter of movement from the chieftain and his family. Was it nervousness? Shame? Kor Phaeron took several paces, changing his perspective, his words now coming through instinct as he surveyed the camp from a fresh angle.

'Prestige and honour will reward the Faithful.' He indicated his followers, who waited in groups under the shade of the sunsails and on the deck of the mobile shrine. 'The light of the Powers shall fall upon them and all blemish will be removed from the body so that it reflects the purity of the soul.'

From this new position he realised that Fan Morgai had not been looking away *from* Kor Phaeron, but rather the chieftain and his close companions had glanced *towards* something. The main tent at the very centre of the encampment, a large conical structure of white, black and red embroidered with sacred constellations.

* * *

1 2 4

'Plague and misery shall be the lot of the faithless,' said Kor Phaeron, voice dropping to a snarled whisper, his fierce gaze roaming over the crowd, seeking other suspicious behaviours or signs of guilt. 'Nothing is hidden from the gaze of the Powers. All is laid bare before their immortal scrutiny as the desert is set before the blazing sun.'

This garnered a definite reaction, an exchange of looks between Fan Morgai and his wife. Kor Phaeron stepped towards the crowd, arms outstretched with palms facing out as though laying benedictions upon them. They shuffled from his path, parting like sand before the wind, until he came to stand before Fan Morgai. He turned an accusing stare upon the nomad leader.

'What is in your heart, Fan Morgai? When the Powers turn their gaze upon you, shall they see one of the Faithful, or an agent of the faithless?'

Fan Morgai said nothing but swallowed hard, meeting Kor Phaeron's gaze for only a moment. A bead of sweat ran down the side of his face – not unusual in such conditions, but the preacher took it as a further omen of the Powers' desires. He pressed on, stepping past the chieftain, to thrust a hand towards the leader's abode.

'What secrets do you hide in your own sanctum?' he demanded. 'You may think that you can keep your secrets away from the sight of mortals, but the Powers see all. They look into the hearts and minds of men and women as easily as I look into your eye now. Do not sully your tongue and my ears with denials and lies!'

Cowed, hands trembling, Fan Morgai gave another look to his family and nodded. His wife and children gathered close as he moved towards the tent.

'I meant no wrong by it,' he said quietly, stopping at the threshold. 'I intended no offence to the Powers.'

Kor Phaeron nodded in silence, neither accepting nor condemning the statement. He waited, suppressing his eagerness to see what the Declined had concealed from him. It would be archeotech, he was sure of it; something from one of the dead cities made in the time of the Age Before. All such artefacts were supposed to be turned over to the Covenant but many tribes and rival sects hoarded the archeotech for themselves – as did Kor Phaeron, though the Declined were not to know that he was no longer an accepted member of the Covenant. In fact, he traded on that ignorance, assured of the traditional protections offered to a traveller of holy position.

'Bring it forth so that we might see what the Powers already know,' he commanded imperiously, thrusting his finger again towards the tent.

Fan Morgai pulled back the heavy flap of the door and stepped back.

'Come out,' he said with a tremulous voice. 'Don't be afraid.'

Kor Phaeron's already furrowed brow knotted further, confused by this turn of events.

A figure stepped from the tent, with the height and build of a child, swathed in the robes and scarves of a desert dweller. Kor Phaeron was about to demand to be told what was happening when the child turned his face towards the preacher. For an instant he saw violet eyes, as intense as the sun, before the light of the Powers blinded him, ending the universe as it had been, ushering in the Age of the Golden One.

1 3 1

Nairo and a few others broke into a run as the master gave a piercing cry and fell backwards as though struck, hands clutched to his face. Like grass flattened by a wind, the Declined fell to their knees around the tent, the movement rippling outwards to reveal a solitary figure stood in the doorway. Axata, the commander of the guards, a giant of a man from Golgora, bellowed orders to his warriors, sending them into the camp, weapons at the ready.

'Wait, wait!' Nairo shouted, surging in front of the others despite his age-worn limbs.

His fears were unfounded; Axata moved his company only to secure the area, but gave no order to attack. Nairo had eyes only for the master – not out of any loyalty to Kor Phaeron, for he was a despicable man, but for fear of his own future. Without the master, he and the other slaves would be left to the untempered attention of the guards, who would likely be even worse than the preacher.

Nairo was a few strides from the fallen figure of Kor Phaeron before he looked at the figure at the threshold of the tent. In the moment his eyes met the violet gaze of the child all the strength ebbed from his body and his head swam. Mid-stride he fell face-first into the hot sands, senses whirling, the image of a golden face burned into his thoughts.

1 3 2

It sounded like singing at first, as though a chorus from an Empyreal choir away in the distance. A harsher sound entered, the chatter of the silver crows that used to flock in the trees outside the gate of the orphanage. Noise swirled around Kor Phaeron, swaying from one side to the other, dizzying and brutal. It resolved into voices: the desert-cant of the nomads. He knew a few words and phrases of the tongue but recognised nothing that was said.

He opened his eyes, but saw only the darkness of the sunshade for a few heartbeats before the scarf-shrouded, weathered faces of the Declined intruded upon his view, concern in their dark eyes. They receded at a shout from Axata, scattering from the approach of the guardmaster and his armed companions. A few of the slaves crouched over their master, hands outstretched but unwilling to touch his holy flesh.

Pain throbbed across his forehead and pulsed in his temples when he sat up. Blinking hard, he could not dismiss the twin pinpricks of brightness that seemed seared into the centre of his eyes. For a moment his discomfort robbed him of all recollection, but with a gasp the memory returned and he sprang to his feet. He averted his gaze from the boy – a half-year old and no more from what Kor Phaeron vaguely remembered of the height and features of the figure that had so stunned him – and his piercing eyes sought Fan Morgai.

He spied the chief of the Declined tribe close to his tent, conversing conspiratorially with his family. He stepped away as he saw Kor Phaeron rouse himself.

'What heresy is this?' demanded the preacher, advancing on Fan Morgai, spittle flying from his lips. 'What have you sequestered from the light in this camp of blasphemies and darkness?'

'He is just a boy, Kor Phaeron,' retorted the chieftain's wife. 'A child we found in the desert. We saved him from the scorching.'

'Just a boy? Do you not see that the light of the Powers is upon him? Why would you hide him from me, the Bearer of the Word?' Kor Phaeron reached the gaggle of nomads and snatched at the robe of Fan Morgai, dragging him close. 'Would you raise him up as some desert soothsayer? Perhaps a false prophet? Think you to be the captor of another Tezen or Slanat, Khaane or Narag? What falsehoods would you lay in his heart, corrupter?'

'He is just a child,' said Fan Morgai, echoing his wife. He pulled himself away from Kor Phaeron's grasp, careful not to lay his own skin upon what he believed was the blessed flesh of an ordained priest. Kor Phaeron noticed a lack of determination in the chieftain's manner, as if an unspoken doubt troubled his thoughts. The itinerant preacher knew that he had looked upon something great, and he knew with equal vehemence that the child could not be raised by the superstitious, ignorant savages of the Declined. Worse still would be to allow the boy to remain with them and then fall into the clutches of the Covenant or one of the other city-churches.

Even so, there was only so far he could push the traditions of hospitality before Fan Morgai decided his guest was no longer welcome. Kor Phaeron raised his hands, touching his fingertips to his briefly closed eyelids in a gesture of apology.

'Forgive my blindness, Fan Morgai,' he said, in what he hoped was his most conciliatory tone. 'You must know that the child is not of mortal birth.'

'Not... mortal? He is not, you are right. Not as we think it. It is only seventeen days since we found him, preacher, in a glassy crater edgewards of the Catarc Oasis. He was an infant, a babe in arms. Now look at him... A half-year aged in just seventeen days.'

'He should come with me, Fan Morgai. I shall lead him to the Truth. You know it is more than happenstance that we have met this day. Of all the deserts to cross, of all the preachers and tribes to meet, the Powers have placed you and I together in this place, at this moment. A greater work is unfolding around us. You have done your part, kept safe that which the Powers have gifted us. Let me take him, Fan Morgai.'

'Why do you not ask me?'

1 3 3

Kor Phaeron stiffened at the sound of the new voice behind him. Its timbre was childlike, formed by immature vocal cords and a small chest, but its tone put him in mind of the High Acolyte of the orphanage where he had been raised, steeped in considered wisdom and calm temperament. It was a voice filled with dignity, speaking perfectly the waterwords. Kor Phaeron met the gaze of the nomad leader and recognised the look in his eye – an understanding of the shock that currently bewitched the holy wanderer. 'I know exactly how you are feeling,' Fan Morgai's expression said to him.

'It is all right, you can look at me now,' the boy said quietly.

Kor Phaeron turned his head and glanced over his shoulder, expecting the blaze of energies that had assailed him before. Instead he saw the boy swathed in shirt and trousers too big, face framed by a dark red scarf. The violet eyes were as bright as before, but there was none of the Empyreal abyss into which

Kor Phaeron had found himself dragged when he had previously met their stare. Even so, the gaze of the child was disquieting. The preacher turned fully to look at the infant but could not find the words he desired. The aura of the boy was intoxicating, a vessel for the Light of the Powers.

'What did you say, Lorgar?' said Fan Morgai.

'You named him?' Kor Phaeron directed a venomous glare at the nomad. 'You gave him one of your filthy sand-names?'

'It is a good name,' Fan Morgai replied. 'A very old name. It came to me the moment I laid eyes upon him. Or, I should say, the moment I recovered my senses after seeing him. It means the *rain-caller.*'

'I like it, Kor Phaeron,' said Lorgar. 'If it does not displease you too much, I should like to keep it. As a reminder of this time with Fan Morgai and his kindness.'

The request was made quietly, but it entered Kor Phaeron's thoughts with the same weight as the commands of the Powers themselves. To deny it would be to attempt to hold back the energy of the sun with his bare hands.

He nodded, struck dumb for a moment.

'A reminder?' Kor Phaeron latched on to the meaning of the words. 'You will accompany me?'

'Your speech was very moving, Kor Phaeron. I know that I am different. Unique. You are the Bearer of the Word, and I would learn of the Powers and the Truth.' He spoke the words with the same inflection as Kor Phaeron, perfectly mimicking the emphasis the priest placed upon them. 'I think that if I am taught of these then perhaps I may understand myself. You can teach me these things.'

'I...' Fan Morgai had tears in his eyes but nodded at this pronouncement, as powerless to resist the boy's desire as the dunes are to resist the shaping of the winds.

* * *

1 3 4

Kor Phaeron felt something else stir in his breast as he looked at Lorgar. The flame of passion burned as never before, ignited by the presence of the child. But in the fire he felt a different purpose than before. When he had been cast into the desert he had vowed to Bear the Word to all who would listen, every convert a reward in itself, proof that he did the works of the Powers and that the Covenant was built upon falsehood and dogma. Now Lorgar presented a new means by which the Word might be elevated. Kor Phaeron's thoughts buzzed with a grander plan, a triumphant return to Vharadesh with a new Prophet beside him to scour clean the corruptions of the Covenant.

He tilted his face away lest something of his desires were shown to Lorgar. Stepping past Fan Morgai, the preacher turned his back on the boy and beckoned impatiently for him to follow across the shadowed sands to the temple-rig.

'Come with me, Lorgar. I will teach you of the Powers and the Truth.'

Growls and grumbles followed them, but no overt protest was made by the Declined. The slaves who had come to their master's aid scurried past, dashing through the heat of the sun to either side to reach the temple-rig ahead of Kor Phaeron. Axata fell into step at his left shoulder.

'Others would kill for the child,' Kor Phaeron told his captain without looking round. 'He is salvation and damnation. Even though they are willing to give him unto us, these vagrants will happily flap their lips of what has occurred here and others will come looking for Lorgar. We cannot have news of the boy reaching the ears of the Covenant. They would scour the desert for us.'

'I understand, holy master,' replied Axata. He peeled away, leaving Kor Phaeron and Lorgar to approach the shrine wagon.

Kor Phaeron waited at the bottom of the ladder and then motioned for Lorgar to precede him up to the deck. When the boy was halfway up, Kor Phaeron grabbed the rungs and hauled himself onto the rig as the sigh of windbows and crackle of fusils burst into life behind him, greeted by the panicked shouts of the Declined.

1 4 1

Though the brightness that had assaulted Nairo's senses had dissipated, the boy, Lorgar, still shimmered with a strange gleam of power – the slave considered the possibility it was simply an effect of a quick onset of desert-fever, for he had fallen out of the shade of the sunsails and had returned to consciousness beneath the furnace heat of the Long Noon sun.

He waited for the master and his new charge to reach the shrine wagon, pausing beside the water butt to refresh them once they had ascended. His hand stopped short of the ladle when the first shots rang out over the camp. From his position on the deck of the temple-rig he saw the sparkle of fusils slash through the shade accompanied by the blur of arrows and slingstave bullets. Larger projectiles, flame-stars and spear-launcher javelins, crashed and whipped into the canopies of the encampment, pulping and piercing those who had incurred Kor Phaeron's wrath.

He tore his eye from the bloody spectacle to see what Lorgar made of the sudden violence. Nairo expected dismay or shock, anger even, but the child placidly watched the unfolding scene, showing not even the smallest evidence of perturbation.

If there was anything to be read in Lorgar's expression it was a slight regret, perhaps, a tilt of the head and purse of the lips that made Nairo wonder if the child had been expecting this outcome. He seemed remarkably unflustered by all the other events that had swept up around him, and there was something knowing about his manner, far beyond his years.

The master pushed the child towards the ladder and bade him climb. Beyond, Kor Phaeron's guards now had blades and mauls in hand, hacking and clubbing down the last of the Declined. Some were already dragging the nomads' belongings from the tents, setting fire to the emptied pavilions; others were leading the sternbacks and sunstriders out of their corral to be added to the beasts of the caravan.

It was not the first time Nairo had seen such acts and he knew that by the time rest-eve had passed the bodies would be buried by the sands, the ashes scattered by the winds, the smoke dispersed into the upper airs, and nothing would remain of Fan Morgai and his tribe. Their souls the Powers would reward or punish as they saw fit – likely subjected to everlasting torture in retribution for a lifetime of faithlessness if Kor Phaeron's lectures were to be believed.

Lorgar reached the top of the ladder and Nairo proffered a hand to help him through the gap in the gunwale. He hesitated, about to pull back his fingers before they touched the unnatural child. Their eyes met again and Nairo read curiosity in the violet gaze. He remembered it was a boy who ascended, not one of the Powers, and gripped his wrist to pull him over the threshold.

1 4 2

The child, still swathed in his nomad clothing, almost fell onto the deck, righting himself at the last moment with a fierce grip on the shawl of Nairo. Kor Phaeron hauled himself through the opening just after, darting an irritated look at the slave.

'Water,' he snapped, flicking a finger towards the keg. 'I am as parched as the Lancaxa Sandstraits. Now!'

Nairo dipped the ladle into the water and filled a metal cup for his master, offering with eyes averted. He heard Kor Phaeron take three large gulps, droplets pattering to the deck, evaporating almost immediately despite the shade of the awning above. The cup was thrust back into his hand and Nairo looked up. He moved to fill it again, for the boy, but Kor Phaeron shook his head.

'He does not drink yet.'

'Who are these people?' Lorgar asked, looking at the slaves going about their various tasks.

'The forgotten, the unclean, the unworthy,' said Kor Phaeron. 'Slaves.'

'And what do they do?'

'Whatever I demand of them.'

Lorgar absorbed this information without gesture or comment, but his brow creased slightly beneath the ragged edge of his head scarf.

'And what did they do to deserve such treatment?'

Kor Phaeron grimaced and loomed over the child.

'Firstly, child, you will address me as "my master", or "Bearer of the Word". Secondly, you will not ask questions until invited to do so. I will teach you the Truth – concern yourself only with such lessons as I deem right. I will indulge you a moment longer, as you are new to the path of enlightenment.' The preacher pointed at Nairo and swept his finger across the rig to encompass the others who had been made out-caste. 'They are slaves because they offended the Powers.'

'And who arbitrates such offences, my master?' Lorgar asked, innocence radiating from his face. 'For how long is the punishment administered?'

'You misunderstand, Lorgar. You must learn to pay more attention if you are to seek the Truth. They are slaves, a miserable position to be in, so one must conclude that in order to suffer such a fate the Powers must be punishing them. You heard my sermon. To each a path is shown by the Powers and each will walk it as the Powers desire. They are slaves because the Powers wish it to be so. If the Powers no longer desire them to be slaves, they will find fresh positions and freedom. It is not in the judgement of mortals to inflict or release such bondage.'

Lorgar accepted this wisdom with a thoughtful look. Nairo saw no compassion in the boy's strange eyes, but there was also none of the coldness and disdain of the guards, nor the venom and cruelty of Kor Phaeron.

'Master?' Nairo touched his fingertips to his eyes as apology for the interruption. 'Where is Lorgar to sleep? To eat? Will he stay with you? Or billeted with the guards?'

The master considered the question for a moment before a flicker of a sly smile twisted his lips.

'He will eat, sleep and pray with your kind, Nairo. He will attend higher lessons when I call for him, without delay. If he is tardy you will all be punished. And get him out of those stinking Declined rags. I'll not have my pupil dressed as a faithless sand rat. You will find proper acolyte's garb in my largest chest.'

Nairo acknowledged his instructions with a nod and a knuckle to his forehead.

'Am I to be a slave, my master?' asked Lorgar. As with everything thus far, the wondrous child seemed intrigued rather than afraid, angered or perplexed.

'That is the first aspect of the Truth you must understand, Lorgar,' Kor Phaeron replied. He put two fingers together in the gesture of blessing but pointed them to the heavens, at the pale disc of the sun that could be seen through the weave of the awning. 'We are all slaves beneath the gaze of the Powers.'

1 4 3

Kor Phaeron retired to his rooms to continue his studies while Axata and his warriors finished the cleansing of the Declined. Nairo, when his many labours gave him brief opportunity, observed Lorgar on a box at the rail watching the execution and dismantling. He seemed even younger dressed in the simple pale smock of a Covenant acolyte, the golden skin of his arms exposed. With headscarf removed his scalp was revealed, with not a single hair upon it. It glistened with sweat despite the shade of the awning.

Corpsehawks had started to descend from the high thermals and the sands shifted and bulged around the footprints of the mercenary Faithful as subterranean scavengers moved through the desert, both drawn by the blood leaking into the dunes. The boy seemed not to notice this activity, his gaze in constant motion, shifting from one person to the next, only briefly dwelling for any time on an individual.

Sanding brick in hand, Nairo made his way along the deck and started to work at the timbers near the boy, chafing away weathered paint with circular strokes. He kept his voice quiet when he spoke, though only a handful of the master's guards were on deck while the grim eradication of the Declined continued.

'What are you looking for, Lorgar?' Nairo asked.

'Everything, Nairo,' the child replied with a solemn expression, not turning around. 'I am trying to see it all but there is too much.'

'All of what? And how do you know my name? The master made no introductions.'

'I heard all of your chatter as you approached the camp, and everything that has been said since I came aboard. I know all of the names that have been spoken, though I cannot put them all to people yet. The one there…' He pointed to a Cathracian in the camp, wearing a tight-fitting purple jerkin and black leggings, her long hair tied with dozens of silk ribbons of the same colours, loading pillaged jewellery onto a sandsled. 'She is called Artharas. She curses frequently, and she looks many times at that one, the Cthollic female Corshad. She desires her more than the gems she collects. There is another called Fabbas who is also talking much about Corshad's body, but he is below decks and I have not yet seen him.'

'You see and hear all of that?' Nairo could not help but stare in wonder at Lorgar. 'It is as though you see their hearts. Their souls.'

'Is that possible?' Now the child glanced down at Nairo, excited. 'These are just the movements on the surface. Sounds and light. Can one really see a soul?'

'I think so,' said Nairo. 'What else of yours could it be that blinded us?'

'I do not know,' Lorgar replied sadly. 'The Declined said that I was a watergift, but Kor Phaeron believes I am from the Powers.'

'He does?'

'I hear him muttering to himself in his cabin below our feet,' said the boy. 'He has fallen silent, just breathing.'

'He is likely reading,' said Nairo. 'Searching the texts for inspiration.'

'Will the texts explain what I am? Kor Phaeron promised that I will learn the Truth. I think that means I will learn what it is I am. I know I am not a child of humans – I saw the infants of the Declined and they are not like me.'

'The Covenant has many lessons and prophecies, and the stories of the prophets are full of messages from the Powers.

If any man or woman can decipher their meaning it will be the Bearer of the Word.'

Lorgar said nothing else and returned his attention to the camp of the nomads, but Nairo noticed a small furrow in his brow as his eyes resumed searching the faces of the converts.

1 4 4

They left the remnants of the Declined and continued into the desert, pressing on through rest-eve while Kor Phaeron spent time in his cabin, agitated by his discovery, attempting to divine its meaning with meditation and prayer. The relentless Long Noon heat dipped into wake-rise and wake-main of Post-noon, and when they had slept again the caravan began its preparations for Duskeve, heralded by a drop in the winds from the outlands that left the temple-rig's bunting lank and limp on the masts and rails.

At the very moment of the wind's last breath, almost to the horn call as wake-rise became wake-main, Kor Phaeron appeared at the gangway from the lower deck. He looked to the lowering sun, face shielded by one raised hand, a bronze-bound tome in the other. The lookouts at the mastheads signalled a clear horizon with pennants of red. Return flags of the same fluttered on the standard poles of the outriders.

At a nod from Kor Phaeron, the address system blared into life, a crackling note that summoned his Faithful to the dusk mass. With practised care, the land yachts tacked back towards the temple-rig while the great machine snarled and growled as brakes were applied, gears slipped and the engines forced into idleness. The other chariots, buggies and trikes of the caravan pulled alongside, forming an oval laager around the vehicle of their spiritual lord.

The crews drew out their prayer shawls of brightly dyed wool, and assembled on the deck of the shrine wagon and on the cooling sands around it. They drew the heavy shawls over their heads and shoulders and knelt, protected from the still considerable power of the sun.

Kor Phaeron ascended to the lectern pilaster and looked over his gathering, seeing them as a mass rather than as individual slaves and converts. His eye was drawn to the small form of Lorgar, knelt among the slaves at the back of the congregation. The child stared up at Kor Phaeron with his keen gaze, drinking in every detail, boyish features lit on one side by the slowly setting sun.

The preacher tried to push the youth from his thoughts, to bring forth the words with which he addressed the coming night.

1 4 5

'Now the peace of the eve is upon us.' His words carried the length of the caravan via the speaker system. 'We are at transition.'

'Transition,' chorused the assembly, the higher pitched voice of Lorgar a heartbeat later than the others, as he copied their response at a nudge from Nairo on his left.

'This is the time of calm reflection. To consider the acts of the day and the duties of the night. The burning sun gives way to the cold stars. The Powers do not slumber though their blazing eye is turned elsewhere, for in the vaults of the Empyrean above they show us the path on which we must travel.'

Kor Phaeron turned towards the coming night and held out his open hand. A solitary light twinkled in the distance just above the horizon.

'Behold the First Star, night eye of the Powers, the guide.'

'The guide,' whispered the congregation, again with the jarring echo of Lorgar's late but enthusiastic intonation. Kor Phaeron pressed on despite the disruption.

'Across the Empyrean the Powers have scattered their messages.' He held up the heavy tome in his hands, the *Book of Heavenly Scripts*, proffering it to the invisible Powers above. 'As we transition from day to night, heat to chill, action to contemplation, I shall consult the oracles of the skies and seek the Truth.'

'The Truth.' This time Lorgar's timing was almost perfect, though whether out of instinct or earlier prompting by his companions, Kor Phaeron could not know. He placed the *Book of Heavenly Scripts* on the lectern and suppressed a sigh as he considered the day's events.

There was no point hiding from the fact that it had been a remarkable day. If he said nothing regarding Lorgar the converts and slaves would simply fill the void with their own superstitious musings. Better to set the tone from the outset and establish his authority.

'Today we have witnessed a marvel.' He motioned for Lorgar to rise. 'Stand up, child.'

Lorgar rose as commanded, swamped by the heavy shawl of many colours that one of the slaves had given to him. Even so, there was undeniable strength and dignity in his poise.

'The Powers delivered unto us this boy. Lorgar. We saved him from a questionable fate at the hands of the desert savages. Do not be fooled by outward appearance. They are the Declined, unworthy to even set foot within the cities of Colchis. Their souls have been touched by faithlessness, their families and ancestors cursed to roam the wilderness for their sins.

'And that curse would have leaked into the soul of Lorgar had he remained with them. It is our turn – our right! – to raise him in the ways of the Truth. I shall be his master, but we must all be his teacher. I am the Bearer of the Word, but we all must bear the burden of his education.

'Think on this for the hour of contemplation. Remember that the Powers have given us this time to ponder the mysteries of their universe, and one such mystery has entered our lives this day.

'Lorgar, you have many questions, but the answers you seek will only be found through study, obedience and adherence to the edicts of the Truth. Tonight I shall begin your instruction in astromancy so that in time you too shall discern the wisdom and missives of the Powers, but first you must learn the scriptures of our forebears.'

Kor Phaeron waved for Lorgar to kneel again and then raised his hands to the Empyrean, eyes closed. He took a moment to give silent thanks to the Powers for this boon, for though he had tried to remain strong after his castigation and exile, and though the light of the Powers fell upon him each day, he knew they could see the doubts that had assailed his thoughts of late.

Lorgar was reward for his perseverance, confirmation that he was still on the correct course across the wildlands of the Powers' arcane design. He needed no surer sign of his destiny than that which had been sent to him clad in the guise of a child: a pupil ready to be enriched with faith and the Truth. What else would better show the people of Colchis that a new age had dawned, an age with the Covenant broken down and rebuilt by the hand of the great Kor Phaeron?

He opened his eyes, feeling the strength of the Powers radiating afresh from his body, invigorated by their blessing. His followers looked to him, ready and willing to do his bidding, eyes bright and hungry for his Lore and his Law. Unto him they had placed their souls and he would not fail them.

Receiving his nod, as one they chanted together.

* * *

146

Great Powers, dwellers in the Empyrean,
Hear today our thanks for thy creation,
And thy merciful aversion of thy divine wrath at our trespasses.

King of Storms, Lord of Blood,
Hear today our thanks for thy strength,
And thy protection from the conquests of the impure.

Queen of Mysteries, Lady of Fate,
Hear today our thanks for thy knowledge,
And thy watchfulness against the hazards of uncertainty.
Prince of Hearts, Sire of Dreams,
Hear today our thanks for thy inspiration,
And thy indulgences of our mortal ambitions.

Princess of Life, Mother of Hope,
Hear today our thanks for thy vigour,
And thy generosity in times of need and austerity.

Praise be to the prophets.

Praise Khaane!
Praise Tezen!
Praise Slanat!
Praise Narag!

1 5 1

Kor Phaeron's cabin was sparsely furnished, more austere even than those of the senior converts. It was not that he considered it a moral choice to keep it so – he possessed a few luxuries such as the blanket of softest capricor wool and the stash of Nomorian chocolate he had been eking out since his escape from that city – but more a matter of necessity and habit. He had possessed nothing but the rags on his back when he had been ejected from Vharadesh and the experience had taught him to travel lightly.

The books took pride of place in a cabinet that was in fact two travelling cases attached to the wall. If he was required to leave in haste they were all that he needed to take with him, assuming that he had opportunity to do so – he was not so admiring of the Powers that he would lay down his life for handwritten and printed pages and an old crystal reader.

The window and shutter were propped open by a forked branch from a woundbark tree, which had served as his rod of office for nearly half a year until a tribal leader had gifted him the old sceptre that hung over his bed. The haft of the rod was still lined with the thick red sap from which the tree's name was derived. Through the window, the twilight crept over the bare metal of the rig's underbelly and onto plain wooden walls. More light came from a small lumen cube on an upturned crate beside the cot, as well as primitive tallow-lights on other shelves.

The flickering gleam caught on old circuit boards and chipped reader gems. A few other ornaments of no particular physical value were stored in open boxes on the floor, mostly gifts from thankful audiences or offerings to the Powers that Kor Phaeron had intercepted before they had been thrown into burials, sacrifice pits or ritual furnaces.

Kor Phaeron sat on the cot with the *Book of Heavenly Scripts* open upon his lap, thumbing through the pages of the prophetic almanac until he found those that pertained to the current season.

'My master?'

Lorgar's inquiry made him flinch. The child had not made a sound as he had descended the steps.

'Knock upon the door!' snarled Kor Phaeron. 'Never enter my chamber unbidden.'

'I am sorry, my master. The Declined live in tents, there is no surface upon which to knock.' The apology seemed sincere even tempered as it was by excuse. Lorgar's fingers moved to his eyes in the gesture of contrition, somewhat uncertainly, unsure whether it was appropriate at that moment. 'I am here for my first lesson, my master.'

'Kneel here.' Kor Phaeron pointed at the floor between the door and the cot. Lorgar obeyed. The preacher stood and slid the *Book of Heavenly Scripts* back into the space upon the chest-shelf and took down the *Instructions on the Lessons of Dammas Dar.*

'Am I to learn to read, my master?'

Kor Phaeron's backhanded slap caught the boy across the

cheek, leaving the skin reddened, though also a throbbing in the bones of the preacher's hand. Lorgar's head had barely moved with the blow but his eyes were wide and tear-filled from shock.

'I gave no permission for questions, child,' Kor Phaeron said coldly, nursing his knuckles. 'If you cannot accept simple instruction I will not waste my time with you. Attend to my words and leave aside your own.'

'Yes, my master,' replied Lorgar, head lowered, lip trembling.

'You will learn to read and write in time, but first you must be taught the principles of faith.' He opened the book to the title page, tracing the words as he read out loud, each fastidiously copied by hand from the original text written in the Age Before. 'Instructions on the Lessons of Dammas Dar. Translated from the Epicean by Kap Daeron of Vharadesh. Third Imprinting. Vharadesh University Press.'

1 5 2

Coldfall was nearing rest-eve, the better part of wake-main spent in reading. Kor Phaeron's neck ached. He flexed his shoulders and looked up to see Lorgar staring intently, soaking in each word with penetrating eyes. The preacher could also read the already familiar furrow at the bridge of the nose that marked Lorgar's face before he made an inquiry. Yet for all that he obviously desired to ask something he held his tongue. Kor Phaeron chose to reward this display of discipline.

'What do you wish to know, child?'

'The Declined spoke of Vharadesh as though it were a place of devils and murderers. Yet you have a book from there.'

'Is there a question in that?'

'Tell me more of Vharadesh, my master.'

'No. Today is not a lesson in geography or history. You need only know that Vharadesh is both the paradise of the Powers and the hell of mortals. It is the capital of the Covenant, blessed in the light and plunged into the abyss for their ignorance. One day we shall travel there, you and I, but it shall not be as supplicants again. Ill-favoured for Vharadesh will be that day. The Covenant must fall so that the Covenant might rise again in the light of the Truth.'

Lorgar opened his mouth but closed it again, stifling the next question that had risen in his thoughts. The boy clenched his jaw as though the words were physically fighting to escape him.

Kor Phaeron's glare forestalled any further struggle and the boy fell into acquiescent immobility. Still regarding Lorgar with an injunctive stare, the preacher turned the page and then started to read once more.

The book was not the prayers and prophecies of the Epicean himself, but a summary and examination of them. Unfortunately Kor Phaeron had never seen the original text on which the book remarked, but he had inferred much of Dammas Dar's observations nonetheless.

As he continued to read aloud he became uncomfortably aware of Lorgar's scrutiny. The boy's gaze moved between the face of the preacher and the book in his hands, his jealousy plain to see.

'You desire this?' snapped Kor Phaeron, slamming the book shut to thrust it into Lorgar's face. 'You think you will find your answers in here without my help?'

'No, my master,' Lorgar pleaded, holding up his hands in submission. 'Forgive my trespasses, my master, as we pray the Powers forgive them. I desire only to understand. Please, read me more of the *Instructions on the Lessons of Dammas Dar.*'

'Do not make demands of your teacher, child.' Kor Phaeron stood up, blanketing the boy in his shadow. 'Do you think to know what is best for you? Perhaps I should have left you with the ignorant sand rats?'

Lorgar said nothing in response to this accusation, his lips tightening against a rebuke that went unspoken. The thought alone enraged Kor Phaeron; that this waif he had saved from destitution and damnation would gainsay his wishes?

'Wake-main is near spent, and the observations of the Empyrean must commence shortly. What have you learned, Lorgar? Why should I not consign you to the slaves' lot and leave you to grub what you can of the Truth from my sermons?'

'"In the first instance, we can summarise the attitudes of Epicea and its people as one of platitudes rather than adulation, as evidenced by the need for Dammas Dar to speak out against the rites of the Crimson Temple,"' began Lorgar, perfectly repeating the opening lines of the text. '"We shall investigate the origins of this protest in the initial chapters. When we have established the platform from which Dammas Dar was st–"'

1 5 3

'Enough!' growled Kor Phaeron. He seized the collar of Lorgar and made to drag the child to his feet. For two heartbeats nothing happened; the boy remained exactly where he knelt as the acolyte's tunic stretched in Kor Phaeron's spindly fingers. And then Lorgar rose, seemingly only by his volition, though the child was of no size to contest the preacher's strength – even given that Kor Phaeron was not himself a muscular individual.

'Do not echo my words back at me, child! It is a mockery of the lesson.'

He propelled Lorgar to the door and then out to the steps in the corridor beyond, slapping his hand upon the back of Lorgar's head to urge him to the deck.

'My master, I heard every word!' protested the boy. He sobbed between the preacher's blows and tried to continue with his recitation. '"In chapters seven and eight we shall endeavour to unpick the tapestry of exaggeration the Epicean wove around the events during the siege of Gall Tassara, to see if we might extract some semblance of reality from the fanciful." Are these not the words you spoke, my master?'

They reached the harshly illuminated deck and Kor Phaeron put his bare foot to the rump of the boy to send him stumbling into the light, though the impact jarred his knee and hip. The guards and slaves roused from their idling and labours to see what was happening.

'You speak but say nothing!' roared Kor Phaeron. 'You think to make an idiot of me by learning the words but not the meaning. It is not the mere rote of the phrases that you will learn, but the inner Truth. The Covenant would bury our world with ceremony and holy cant, but we will die of it as a man in the desert dies of lack of water, for there is no faith in blind devotion, no Truth in the word spoken out of thought. I will not be tasked in this way by an acolyte.'

Lorgar stood trembling, clutching at his tunic, but Kor Phaeron knew that an example had to be made right now. The boy, and those who watched, needed to learn that only true faith would serve the Powers. He would not raise an automaton like the academies of Vharadesh, but an acolyte of the Truth.

'Axata, bring your lash here,' he said, gesturing to the commander of the converts. 'If Lorgar will not heed my words, chastisement will make a deeper impression.'

Axata approached, uncoiling the whip from his belt. Kor Phaeron sneered at the man's caution and thrust a finger towards Lorgar.

'Make the marks upon his flesh so that the Truth might make marks upon his soul!'

* * *

154

In the darkness of the below deck, the boy's startling eyes glistened and tears cut tracks through the grime on his face. Lorgar huddled close to a thickly riveted stanchion, eyeing Nairo with suspicion. The slave had cleared the others out of the room to give the child some privacy, and stood protectively at the bulkhead, the door behind him opened a hand's width to let in a sliver of light from the corridor outside.

'I... I did... I learned the words, Nairo,' Lorgar said, choking out the words between sobs. His eyes roamed the gloom for a moment and then settled again on the slave, lost and confused. 'I remembered them perfectly! I thought he would be pleased. Why was he so upset?'

'I don't know, Lorgar,' Nairo confessed. 'The master is sometimes swift to take affront but very slow to offer explanation.'

He held out a hand, laid it carefully on the boy's arm so as not to startle him.

'Let me see,' he said softly.

Lorgar shuffled away and shook his head.

'No.'

'Where does it hurt?'

'In here,' Lorgar said, tapping his exposed chest. He raised quivering fingers to his forehead. 'In here.'

'What of your back? Six blows Axata put upon you.' In a crouch, Nairo moved closer, tugging gently at the tunic. 'Let me check the wounds.'

Lorgar darted him a scared look, but Nairo smiled as reassuringly as his gap-toothed mouth allowed, nodding encouragement.

'I'll not touch anything. Just let me see.'

Reluctantly, Lorgar nodded, turning so that his back came into the light. Nairo slipped away the tunic, exposing the boy's shoulders and upper spine. In the dim light he could barely see half a dozen red welts running diagonally across the middle of his back and left shoulder. He turned and pushed the door open a little wider to let in more light, but this did not reveal any further damage. There was not even a scab to show where the whip cracks had landed.

'No grazing, no bruises. The skin isn't broken at all…' Nairo shook his head in disbelief. 'I think perhaps you have an ally in Axata, and he laid the whip on you less harshly than it seemed. I thought it odd you did not cry out. Perhaps you need to be as good an actor as he is, for I would swear he put his arm into every blow. Cover up, lest the master sees the lack of injury. He would not like to think that Axata has spared you the full application of chastisement, and it would bode poorly for both of you.'

Lorgar shrugged the tunic back on and turned to Nairo.

'It does not hurt, not there. My soul is injured, Nairo. The ache is in my hearts.'

'You mean heart, Lorgar. Just the one.'

The boy scowled and shook his head.

'I can hear your heart, Nairo. And that of Dervas on the deck above, and many others. I know you only have one heart. But listen to mine.' He waved for the slave to bow his head to Lorgar's chest and Nairo did so, hesitantly, until his ear came upon his slender breastbone.

He heard an unmistakable twin-beat pulsing through the bone and sat bolt upright, staring at Lorgar with fresh amazement. The boy smiled, thrilled by this small surprise.

'I told you!' he grinned.

1 5 5

Nairo wondered what other marvels were hidden in the body of the child, but said nothing. There had been something unsettling in the way he had meekly submitted to his punishment, crying but not struggling, not protesting. His soul was as special as his body, that much was evident. The master had been right – the Powers had set Lorgar upon this world for a purpose. A fifth prophet, perhaps? But for whom? A new Power? The thought both excited and terrified Nairo in equal measure.

Lorgar laughed and pointed at the slave.

'See? Your heart, it beats faster now. Thud-thud. Thud-thud. I can hear it like the footsteps of Dagaron the Capazcian pacing the deck above.'

Nairo listened and could hear only the creaking of the metal and the judder of the engines idling to keep the generators going. Yet he did not doubt the boy's testament. He could no more stop the racing of his heart at the thought of what the child represented than he could hold back the desert winds.

'Rest here until the master summons us for the observations,' he told the boy as he turned to leave.

'Nairo...'

The slave looked back.

'I could learn the words more quickly if I did not have to wait for Kor Phaeron to read them.'

'You can read the books?' Nairo had thought that he could not be any more surprised by anything else he learned of the boy, but was mistaken, as he would be about a great many things in the coming years.

'Not yet, but I'm sure it wouldn't take long to learn, would it?'

'For you...?' Nairo shrugged. 'Probably not. But Kor Phaeron lets no other read his holy books. You must be patient and attend to his lessons and his instructions. Be diligent – the slightest trespass might incur his anger.'

'But if I could just get–'

'No!' Nairo turned back fully and held up a finger in admonishment. 'Put such thoughts from your mind, Lorgar. Do not disobey the master. It will go badly.'

'But perhaps you–'

'If he caught you, his acolyte, you would be beaten. If he caught me taking one of his books. Me, a slave... My hands would be forfeit. My life, most likely, taken in a painful and drawn-out way.'

'I thought you wanted to help,' Lorgar said with a pout.

'When did I say that?'

'You did not say it, not with words. But you are here, now, and others are not. Thank you.'

Nairo retreated, not acknowledging the praise nor the boy's assessment of his spirit, for he knew that as much as he could not let the boy needlessly suffer, he also harboured a secret, grander hope. The boy's favour. With it, who could say what might yet be achieved for the likes of a slave?

'Nairo?'

The question stopped him just at the threshold, but he did not look back.

'Is there ever not a question upon your lips, Lorgar?'

'You speak well, better than the other slaves. I think you can read, also. You were not born into slavery, were you? What did you do before... before becoming a slave?'

He was not going to answer at first, but there was something undeniable about Lorgar's questions, about his voice, that meant one could not disobey nor ignore his request.

'A teacher. I was a teacher, of sorts, before I was made a slave.' He heard the boy take in a breath, ready to speak, and guessed at the next query. 'I was enslaved for teaching the wrong thing, to the wrong people, if that is what you want to know.'

'And what was that?'

Nairo gritted his teeth, trying to refuse the urge to comply. It was more than simply the child's voice prising open his volition; it was his desire to speak that made him do so, to share that secret.

'Freedom, Lorgar. A heresy in the eyes of the Covenant. I taught that all men and women were equal beneath the gaze of the Powers.'

And that was more than Nairo had been willing to share. If such a thing became known to Kor Phaeron his former identity might be guessed and his life would be forfeit; so before he admitted more, he fled.

161

The incident with Lorgar left Kor Phaeron's patience worn thin, and knowing his own nature the preacher secluded himself in his dorm through rest-eve until the next astromantic observations were required at the break of wake-rise on High Night. He sat on his cot and stared out at the dark desert, waiting for the Powers to pull the thickest veil of night over the skies.

The temperature had dropped rapidly as the heat of the day faded through Coldfall. Here, at one of the highest points of the Vhanagir desolation, snow was more common than rain, but it was not yet the season for such bounty from the Powers. The High Night winds had not yet started, but it would not be long before they brought their chilling touch. Near cloudless, the air would not trap the heat of the day, and well before the close of wake-rise the thermometer would be close to freezing.

Through the caravan the slaves were making ready for the cold, lighting fireboxes and dragging out the solar collectors that had been storing the sun's energy since dawn on Mornday. Parasols that had shielded them from the deadly sun were now reversed, their reflective sides turned inwards to trap as much escaping heat as possible.

The paradox seemed appropriate. Kor Phaeron took up the fitfully glowing screen of an auto-scriber and pressed his thumb to the relic's activation rune.

'We must forever desire the gaze of the Powers,' he said, clearly, slowly so that the diction device could catch each word precisely. A spool of transpex parchment slid out of the end, his words neatly burned onto the surface in a flowing script. The effort of restraining his racing thoughts was a good discipline, helping him shape his philosophy even as he gave voice to it.

'That they have abandoned Colchis is no mystery to me when the Covenant spews mindless rote into the Empyrean, devoid of faith and passion. But to draw the eye of the Powers is to be laid bare to their scrutiny. A testing will come, when we are beset by that immortal gaze once more. Those who hold true to their faith will pass. Those who show weakness of resolve will fail. It is not for mortals to judge but to bring forth the gaze of the Powers and allow their judgement to run its course. When the testing is complete those who remain shall live beneath the invigorating and protective gaze of the Powers once more.'

As he considered these words, Kor Phaeron felt his anger ebbing. He remembered the Truth, that unto each would be given the tasks set to them by the Powers, according to their design. Into him the Powers had invested knowledge of the Truth and the strength to be the Bearer of the Word – the seer among the blind, the listener in a crowd of the deaf, the speaker in a world of mutes. They had entrusted that duty to no other.

But it was so taxing, bearing the responsibility of so many souls.

* * *

1 6 2

Three knocks at the door announced the arrival of a visitor. Axata, Kor Phaeron believed, knowing well the force and pace of his chief convert's request for entry.

'Come in.'

It was indeed the guard captain, his bulk suddenly filling the cabin.

'Sentries posted, patrols sent out, master.'

Kor Phaeron silently nodded his acceptance of the report. He detected a slight awkwardness about his lieutenant's demeanour and his presence was a change from the norm.

'Why do you report in person, Axata? Normally it is sufficient to send word with an underling.'

The giant twisted his hands around the knot of the rope belt that held his acolyte's robe over the plate and mail armour beneath.

'The boy...'

'What of Lorgar?'

'He is not normal. You said so yourself, master.'

'I did.'

'Why is he here?'

Kor Phaeron considered dismissing the question but he could see that the matter would nag at the captain, and through him would infect the thoughts of the other converts. He almost delivered a throwaway platitude, to assure Axata that the Powers had a plan and that they were all a part of it, whether the divine scheme could be seen or not. He stopped himself, knowing that it would be an affront to the Truth. It would be no admission of weakness to share his concerns, and would strengthen Axata's loyalty to think he had been taken into his master's confidences.

'I think his purpose is not for us to divine, but to define, Axata. See how eager he is to learn? He is a mould into which we must pour our faith and our wisdom, to create something beautiful and holy.'

Axata nodded slowly and scratched broken nails across his stubbled chin. He narrowed his eyes.

'But what purpose do you have for him? You teach him like an acolyte, but beat him like a slave.'

'There is greatness in Lorgar, that is plain to see. It must be founded upon humility if it is to be of worth to the Powers. We must put it foremost in his mind that he serves the design of the Powers, not any mortal ambition.'

Again Axata showed his understanding but betrayed further thought with his disturbed expression.

'And what does it mean for us, in particular?'

'For us?' Kor Phaeron chose his next words with care. 'An ending and a beginning, Axata. Lorgar is a sign from the Powers that they have noted our labours. Our exile will end, our time in the wilderness, both literal and figurative, shall one day cease. Lorgar is the key to that future.'

'You intend to destroy the Covenant?'

'I like your quick wit, Axata – that is why you are my right hand. But in this you are wrong. The Covenant is the Church of Colchis, the rightful institution of the Powers. The Covenant is more than the priests and priestesses, the choruses and choirs, the temples and cloisters. The Covenant must endure, but to do so it must also be changed. We shall be that change, Axata, you and I and the others of the true passion. Lorgar has been delivered to us for that end. If you wish to know his purpose, look no further than the walls and spires of Vharadesh. Praise the Powers.'

'Praise the Prophets,' replied Axata. Heartened by these words, he left Kor Phaeron, who was also invigorated by the exchange.

The Truth was simple and Kor Phaeron chided himself for not seeing it earlier. Lorgar's arrival was not a test, it was an opportunity.

1 7 1

High Night came, bitter and clear, when the stars were full-bright. Nairo and the other slaves dismounted from the temple-rig in preparation for the observations, bringing mats and telescopes for the master.

It was cold beneath the cloudless skies, and the slaves pulled tight such rags and cloaks as they had while they waited. Nairo looked up at the constellations. He knew a few, the majors, like any child of Colchis. The Opening Eye, with the red star of Valak as its pupil. The Rising Stair, which looked more like a waterfall to Nairo but who was he to doubt the judgement of the ancients? The Serrated Sun, just above the horizon, called by some the Iron Halo of Khaane.

Almost directly overhead shone the Exalted Gates, through which could be seen the smudge that scholars testified to be the clouds surrounding the mountain of the Empyrean – the Godpeak to which the prophets had conducted the Pilgrimage, whose precipitous and unwelcoming flanks they had ascended into the mists of the Powers.

Nairo had once stolen a look through his master's viewing scope, when Kor Phaeron had been studying the Exalted Gates.

He had seen the distant swirl that concealed the Godpeak and, for a moment, had felt a connection to the Powers. He had known in that moment what Kor Phaeron meant when he said that they dwelt beneath their immortal gaze.

But it was impossible to reconcile that moment with the nature of his existence, nor accept on faith alone that his slavery, that the subjugation of millions, was an intended part of the Powers' design.

'Maska!' His voice was a sharp whisper, his eyes constantly roving back to the rig and the guards upon the masts and at the rail. Not that they were bothered about the slaves trying to escape; any fool who wanted to dare the wilderness alone would shortly be joining the Powers. The deadly desert was more surety against escape than any patrols or fences. Nairo looked for a sign of their master appearing, for he desired no one to overhear his conversation and was reminded of Lorgar's claims of extraordinary hearing.

Maska approached at his furtive but insistent gesturing. Lorra, Baphae and Kal Dekka responded to similarly clandestine summoning, congregating beside the main observational array. They pretended to examine the spokes and gears as they conversed, lips almost motionless, their voices barely audible over the night breeze and flap of cloaks.

'I overheard the master speaking to Axata,' Nairo told the others. 'They intend to raise the boy in the teachings of the Truth, and to return to Vharadesh to use him against the archpriests of the Covenant.'

'Dangerous,' said Baphae, wiping a hand across his beard to obscure his mouth as he spoke. 'If the Covenant hear anything of that they'll hunt us down.'

'There's nothing we can do about it,' said Maska, moving to step away. Nairo caught the hem of her cloak and gently tugged her back.

'You mistake my meaning. Kor Phaeron is to fill Lorgar's head with the Word and the Truth, but perhaps that is not the only thing the boy will learn.'

Lorra darted him a look and then quickly concealed her concern by bending to the mechanism of the main telescope. 'Then it's not the Covenant who'll flay us, but the master.'

'Not if we're careful,' said Baphae. 'Just a lesson here, a lesson there. A bit of compassion maybe.'

'More than that,' whispered Nairo. He took a moment, judging his audience. If he confided his full beliefs they might think him mad, but he could not let the opportunity pass. 'Lorgar could be our saviour. All of us, all Colchisians. Kor Phaeron sort of believes it, though he thinks he will be the vessel of the Powers' return. He'll try to use Lorgar, whatever the boy turns out to be. What if Lorgar really is a fifth prophet? We cannot let Kor Phaeron control that sort of power.'

'Control?' Kal Dekka scoffed. He buffed the barrel of the 'scope with the corner of his tunic. 'If Lorgar is a prophet, nobody will control him, none but the Powers.'

'I can't believe that,' replied Nairo. 'He is just a child at the moment, and a child can be taught, no matter what destiny the Powers have set in store for him. He could be the liberation of us all, the saviour of the slaves.'

'I'd settle for a less lofty goal,' said Maska. 'If he just makes our lives a little easier, I'd be...'

She trailed off, flicking a glance towards the temple-rig before she moved away, attending to other tasks. Nairo glanced over his shoulder to see that Kor Phaeron had emerged onto the deck, bathed in the reflected silvery glow of the stars. He gazed up at the Empyrean and there was an unfamiliar smile upon his face.

Nairo caught Baphae's look, a warning glance. He returned a reassuring wink and hurried back to the shrine wagon to attend to the master's wishes.

* * *

1 7 2

And so the rhythm of the caravan continued, changed in some ways, the status quo retained in others. Each wake-day they traversed the dunes of the great wilderness, guided by the observations of the Coldfall and High Night before. Consulting the stars and the *Book of Heavenly Scripts,* Kor Phaeron divined the Will of the Powers. Where before they had sought out other caravans, heading for the camps of the Declined, oases and wadis, now the master of the temple eschewed his missionary goal, declaring that they must remain hidden from the prying eyes of those who would see the Truth silenced.

Kor Phaeron led the slaves and converts in their prayers and dedications – before breakfast on the cusp of wake-rise, and again before the meal that heralded the transition to wake-main. They gathered, wearing prayer shawls to protect from sun or cold, during the last hour before rest-eve and for brief invocations at the time of sleeping. He spent much time with Lorgar, reading from the texts and instilling his own thoughts into the boy. Lorgar had learned well the lesson of his beating and paid more attention to the substance of the tracts as well as their detail.

He tried hard to keep his questions to himself, but his curiosity was boundless and occasionally his inquisitive nature got the better of his discipline. Sometimes Kor Phaeron indulged these queries if the subject pleased him; other times he called for Axata to apply a short flogging for wasting the master's precious time.

As attested to by the Declined, Lorgar's growth was considerable, so that it seemed each Mornday the fresh sunlight fell upon a youth who was noticeably taller and broader. For one so young he possessed a bulk that would rival Axata one day; his young skin bulged with latent muscle.

His thirst for knowledge was insatiable, and he absorbed all that was passed to him as the sands of the White Plains soak up every drop of rain that falls upon their barren expanse. Lorgar learned quickly, with a fierce appetite not just to understand the texts of the ancients but to hear more of the Age Before: of Colchis, of the Prophets, of the caravans and trade routes. Most of all, though, he longed for stories of the great cities.

It was in this capacity that Nairo and his companions were able to furnish a more rounded education than that provided by Kor Phaeron. Whilst they prepared food, split and spliced cables, cleaned and polished, sawed and hammered, the slaves talked to Lorgar, telling him their tales, sometimes singing the songs of their peoples or sharing the folklore of the desert tribes. While everybody spoke the waterwords as the prescribed cant of the caravan, they each had their own dialects and doggerel. These Lorgar quickly assimilated, and was keen to demonstrate to Kor Phaeron but Nairo warned him not to reveal this to the master. Though dismayed by the thought of subterfuge, Lorgar seemed wary enough of his beatings that he held his tongue and shared his linguistic skills only with the slaves.

At times Nairo spied the youngster listening intently at the hatches or at the base of a mast beneath a guard nest, no doubt paying close attention to the languages of the guards too. Sure enough, after brief study he displayed a remarkable breadth of curses and swear words from three dozen different regions and cities. While this caused a certain amount of hilarity among the converts, who had also secretly started to share their own tales with the boy, it brought swift vocal and physical retribution from the master.

1 7 3

Forty wake-rises and rest-eves passed, by which time Lorgar was almost as tall as Nairo's shoulder, and easily more broad and heavyset. The acolyte frequently engaged in semantic debates with Kor Phaeron, who tested his abilities by hurling doubts and questions that would be used by unbelievers, assuring himself that the child knew the responses to accusations of blasphemy and heresy, to specific arguments against the faith. The boy joked with the converts and slaves, and constructed elaborate fables from their histories, spinning truth into fanciful adventures through the divine realms of the Empyrean.

For Nairo it was a time as back-breaking as ever, but the presence of Lorgar alleviated some of the spiritual pain that he endured. When he saw the boy at prayer he was reminded that hope had returned. Every Dawnaway brought with it the promise of a new future.

Though they did their best to avoid the traders and nomads, eventually their supplies ran low enough to force them back to the more populated tracts of the desert. On the sixth Coldfall after Lorgar's discovery Kor Phaeron consulted the heavenly messengers and asked them to provide guidance. Interpreting the movements above, the master declared that they would head to Ad Drazonti, a nearby oasis.

They set course according to the observations and expected to reach the oasis by wake-main of the coming Mornday. The crew brought up empty water barrels ready for filling before the freeze of High Night made extended labour impossible. Beneath the flickering lumen glare Nairo and others struggled at a pulley and line above the main hatch. He felt a strong hand on his shoulder moving him aside. Lorgar stepped up to the opening and hauled out the keg one-handed, unhooking it from the cable with the other. With ease he stacked it upon the few that had already been raised, and returned to the hatch to send the cable down again. He jumped down into the darkness, where Maska and others fumbled to drag the heavy barrels in the gloom, to hook them up to the winch. Lorgar seemed as keen-sighted as the rats that dwelt in the storage decks, and heaved the barrels to the opening two at a time, before he pulled himself up to the main deck and instructed those below to hang them on the line.

With metronomic repetition the boy laboured, tirelessly and with barely a sweat sheen on his golden skin. Not more than an hour had passed and all of the barrels were stacked along the gunwales.

'What next?' he asked Nairo, clearly invigorated not only by the physical exercise but the practical nature of the task. 'It is rewarding, is it not, to sometimes labour at something measurable? It frees the mind to ponder the greater things. For instance, it has occurred to me whilst I stacked these last dozen barrels that we might consider it a metaphor for our spiritual labours. We can each work as hard as we are able, but only together can we achieve our ends, and as the barrels must be ordered, so too must our thoughts and prayers. The Truth is that we each have a purpose, but it goes beyond that. Not just us, but all things are part of the order of the Powers, to be set aright according to their plan.'

The slave was unsure what to make of it, worried that Lorgar had absorbed too much of the master's demands for hierarchy and subjugation to the will of the Impassioned, as he referred to those who had heeded the Word and allowed the Truth to enter their souls.

'Salting kegs,' Nairo replied after a moment's thought, pointing to the aft hatch. 'We'll be bringing aboard meat.'

Lorgar set to this task with equal vigour, singing hymns that Nairo recognised from *Verbal Offerings in the Temple,* though with extra verses of his own invention. As he rolled the large salting kegs across the deck he regaled his growing audience with 'Glory to the Ascended', but each verse and chorus rendered into a different tongue, effortlessly translated on the fly by the youth as several of the slaves and guards called out for him to use their native dialects next.

1 7 4

It was thus caught up in the festive air that Nairo and the others did not see or hear Kor Phaeron rise from his cabin. The first they realised of his coming was a thunderous bellow as he came into view up the steps from the below deck.

'What is this clownish mockery?'

Converts and slaves scattered like vermin before the lantern, suddenly occupied with tasks in the holds, or engine rooms, or at the far ends of the temple-rig. Lorgar stopped in his tracks, the barrel he had been kicking across the decking rolling to a halt against the gunwale. Nairo stayed close, unable to abandon the boy to face the master's displeasure alone. To his credit, Axata remained also, suddenly hanging his head in shame where moments before he had been cheerfully banging out the beat of the hymn with a fist on the rail.

'You!' Kor Phaeron jabbed a finger towards the guard captain, who flinched as though the accusing digit was the barrel of a fusil. 'Ready your whip!'

The master rounded on the other converts, hectoring and snarling at them to drag forth the slaves who had shirked their duties. They complied quickly, fearing his wrath and that the scorn of the Powers would fall upon them instead. It seemed that it took only moments to round up the thirty-eight men and women, forced to their knees on the deck with Nairo.

'The Powers set us in motion upon the face of the world,' Kor Phaeron spat. 'Unto each of us they have poured their purpose and into their great design they have woven us. If they had desired you to be idle, to giggle and cavort like cliff monkeys, they would not have seen fit to cast you into slavery! Six lashes each.'

1 7 5

Kor Phaeron turned from the slaves having pronounced his judgement, focusing his scorn upon Lorgar. Though almost as big as the master, he quailed from Kor Phaeron's approach as if the Powers themselves had sent an avatar of admonition against him.

'I sought only to help, my master,' the boy explained weakly, all strength and music robbed from his voice.

'It is not your place to help,' Kor Phaeron replied quietly.

The first crack of the whip and yelp heralded the beginning of the punishment for the slaves, but Nairo and those not yet taken in the rough hands of the guards had eyes only for their master and Lorgar. Kor Phaeron spoke calmly, with none of his customary snarling and raging. He seemed disappointed by the boy, genuinely hurt that his acolyte had been so foolish.

'Would you do all of their labours, Lorgar?' Kor Phaeron asked. 'Would you strip the meat from the bones? Stoke the fires? Oil the gears? Wash the clothes? Varnish and paint the temple? Sew the pennants? Sift the sand for landcrabs and beetles and scorpions to cook?'

Lorgar stood dumbfounded, hands gripping each other in front of him, confusion written across his features.

'What of the other slaves, Lorgar?' Kor Phaeron waved a hand past the rail to the darkness of the night. 'Not just those of this caravan, but the others of a hundred traders, a thousand merchants, and the millions in the cities? Would you take all of their labours away? Who would nurse the children? Who would set stone upon stone to erect the monuments to the

Powers? Who would stoke the furnaces and polish the lecterns, and inscribe new copies of the texts? Would you do all of that for them?'

The boy shook his head, shoulders slumped, not looking at his master. The wails of the beaten slaves grew in volume as their punishment continued, the guards working their way towards Nairo. Still he could not turn his gaze from the pair.

'No. No, my master,' Lorgar mumbled.

'No.' Kor Phaeron approached his acolyte, stood a little more than arm's length away. 'So you would decide those you would relinquish of their duties and those who must labour still. You, a mortal, would be the arbiter of who is to slave for others.'

'I...' Lorgar had no reply to this argument. His lip trembled and he glanced at Nairo. His eyes were filled with apology and resignation as Nairo felt unruly fingers clamp on to his shoulder. He looked up to see Carad, one of the Archer Brethren. There was no such pity in her eyes as she pulled the slave to his feet and dragged him towards Axata's waiting lash. Nairo glanced back, imploring Lorgar with a glance, but the boy's expression hardened and he looked back to Kor Phaeron.

'My deepest apologies, my master,' Lorgar said, bowing his head even as Nairo was bent over the rail and the first touch of the whip scored hot pain across the slave's shoulders.

1 7 6

As the punishment continued, Kor Phaeron looked at the line of slaves, their backs bruised and bloodied, and returned his attention to Lorgar. The preacher was pleased that he had kept his temper. It helped to remember that despite his size and intellect, Lorgar was still a child, and whatever abilities the Powers had instilled into him he remained ignorant and innocent in many ways. His actions were not rebellion against Kor Phaeron, simply misguided.

Even so, the fault lay in the compassion as much as the act itself. To feel pity for the slaves was to begin to judge the Powers. If one thought that another did not deserve the lot to which they had been dealt, it was open invitation to other doubts – doubts that could lead to open defiance of the Powers and the Truth. Kor Phaeron knew he would have to be careful, lest Lorgar started seeing the slaves as victims rather than deserving of their suffering.

'Lorgar, attend to me,' he barked, crooking a finger towards the youth.

Lorgar approached along the deck, his expression bereft of suspicion or guile.

'Yes, my master?'

'The slaves have been punished for shirking their duties, but the trespass was not theirs alone.'

'No, my master.' Lorgar hung his head, shame-faced, his bald pate catching the yellow glare of the temple-rig's hanging lanterns. 'It was because of me that they transgressed.'

'You have natural wit and charisma, Lorgar, and others attend to your every word. That is a big responsibility.'

'Yes, my master.'

Kor Phaeron paused a moment, to ensure he phrased his next words properly as he looked down at the child. He did not want to even suggest the possibility that Lorgar might use his emerging abilities for any cause other than that of his master. But it was a delicate subject to broach, for in denying the moral right to do so, Kor Phaeron would introduce the concept itself. At the moment it seemed that the notion of rebellion was not even within Lorgar's mental compass.

'You must swear to me now, an oath upon the Powers.'

'An oath, my master?'

'A promise, witnessed by the Powers, bound to your soul. You will swear by the Powers that you will be a defender of the Truth. You shall take the Word and the Truth to guide you in all things. Upon your immortal soul, give your word to the Powers that all you do shall work to their glory and cause.'

'I do, my master.'

'Say the words, and look to the Empyrean as you declare them. Give your oath fully so that all might hear it, both mortal and those beyond.'

Lorgar glanced at Kor Phaeron and then turned his eyes upwards, his gaze moving to the distant stars.

'I swear… I promise…' Lorgar faltered, uncharacteristically lost for words. He looked to Kor Phaeron with a pleading expression. The moment pleased the preacher greatly, for it served as a reminder that he was the teacher, that Lorgar still had much to learn and only from Kor Phaeron would he receive such tutelage.

'Something like, "I swear by the almighty Powers…" would be a good start. And then say what you promise to do.'

Lorgar smiled and nodded, turning his gaze heavenwards once again.

'I swear by the almighty Powers that… I shall dedicate my life to learning the Word and the Truth, and to serve the Powers as they see fit to guide me. I shall heed their messages from the Empyrean, as they lay them in signs upon the sands and stars, in the minds and hearts of people. All of this I promise, and if I should fail my immortal soul shall be cast from the Empyrean to dwell in the torment of the passionless void.'

1 7 7

'Good,' said Kor Phaeron, feeling a stab of pride at the boy's forthright pronouncement. He saw that the guards and slaves had heard the clear declaration, not only reminding them of the Truth to which they were all subject, but also of Kor Phaeron's authority over Lorgar and, by extension of that, every member of the caravan.

'Now, child, there is the matter of your punishment.'

Again Lorgar nodded his acquiescence, saying nothing. He strode to the rail, stepping past the cowering and moaning slaves. He placed his broad hands upon the metal and bent over, looking to Axata. The converts' captain glanced over to his master for confirmation and Kor Phaeron held up eight fingers in answer.

'Two more lashes than the slaves, Axata, for being the instigator of this sinful exhibition.'

Axata signalled his understanding and readied his whip. Kor Phaeron noticed him exchanging looks with several of his companions, and though it was impossible to know exactly what thought they shared, it seemed to the preacher that they understood how they had been complicit in the debacle. That they had been spared would not pass without remark amongst their ranks, and Kor Phaeron would take time to remind Axata that he also had onerous responsibilities.

Impassively, Kor Phaeron watched as the whip fell across the back of Lorgar, just beneath the shoulder blades. The acolyte's robe absorbed some of the sharp crack, and the boy barely moved. The priest could see nothing of Lorgar's face, but his shoulders were hunched, fingertips digging into the wood of the rail.

'Seven more,' he reminded Axata and turned away to the steps. 'This is a congregation of worship, not a circus.'

1 8 1

A rising Mornday sun brought sight of the oasis at Ad Drazonti. Two pillars of marble rose over the horizon, each topped by a golden beacon fire illuminated by the power of the sun itself – another wonder of the Age Before, that time and the terrible crusades of the past had rendered indecipherable to the wit of even the most learned Colchisian. Like most such watering holes across the vast expanses, Ad Drazonti was seasonal, sometimes in full flood and crowded with dozens of caravans, but at low ebb when the procession of Kor Phaeron arrived in the late wake-rise.

The preacher dispatched the wagons with Axata, crewed by converts and slaves with an apportion of their meagre coinage and the water butts to fill, and the instruction that they needed enough food for at least another seven or eight days; Kor Phaeron wanted as little contact with others as possible.

Using his brass-banded ocular he scanned the oasis, counting three separate missions and caravans at the water's edge. Guard towers, far smaller than the beacon lights, stood in a perimeter several hundred metres further out, delineating the extent of the water hole when it was fully risen. The trees and bushes that thrived on the spring had started to wilt, even this hardy vegetation giving in to the relentless dryness and the unforgiving sun.

Taking the ocular from his eyes, Kor Phaeron spied Lorgar standing at the rail, straining to see what was occurring. He was certain there would be magnoculars and telescopes trained back on their position and the boy was stood in plain view. If his effect on first sighting at the nomad camp was anything to judge by, there was no telling what his presence might stir amongst the more heavily armed trading station and merchant crews.

'Get back below,' snapped the priest as he strode forwards along the deck. 'I said to keep out of sight, you wretched child!'

He seized Lorgar by the collar of his acolyte robe and moved to haul him from the rail. The boy resisted, not moving a centimetre, but the robe pulled away from him. Kor Phaeron stared at the unmarked expanse of Lorgar's broad shoulders where only the passing of High Night before he had been viciously whipped.

'Get below,' he growled, suppressing any further reaction as he propelled the boy towards the hatch to the slave quarters – or attempted to. Lorgar staggered a step and stopped, looking back with a pained expression.

'I want to see the caravans and the guards!' the child protested, forgetting Kor Phaeron's title in his petulance.

Such disobedience had to be suppressed immediately. Kor Phaeron struck the boy across the face, though he felt as if he slapped rock.

'Get below, child,' he snarled through gritted teeth, eyes boring venomously into Lorgar. 'I will deal with this insubordination later.'

Though it was obvious that the blow had caused no real injury, the shock of it and the flare of Kor Phaeron's fury was enough to put the boy to flight, sending him running for the dim spaces below deck.

1 8 2

Kor Phaeron retired to his chamber and brooded, conscious that it seemed Axata had purposefully spared the boy his just punishment. Yet if he moved too far against the leader of the converts, the preacher knew he might find himself abandoned instead. It was time, he considered, that he started elevating another of the converts, fanning the ambitions of one with the lure of replacing Axata if need be.

He spent the rest of the wake-rise considering the candidates until the horns of the address system blared out in greeting to the returning expedition. He stayed below, listening to the rumble of the trucks and the boots on the deck, until all returned to orderliness when the loading of the stores was complete. He waited longer, comforting himself with verses from the *Aspirations of Kor Adras,* reminded by the tribulations of the first high priest of the Covenant that the path to righteousness, the ascent to the peak of the Faithful, was not an easy journey.

Axata's signature knock set his heart thumping at the possibility of the coming confrontation. Kor Phaeron knew that he could not cause open affront to the convert, potentially embarrass him in front of the others, lest he backed Axata into a corner from which the only escape was a fight. No, it would be better to invoke a far higher authority. The Powers themselves. He bade Axata enter and assumed a sombre, regretful expression.

'I have the stores listing...' Axata's report trailed away as he saw Kor Phaeron's sad face. Concern twisted his features as he stepped forwards with a hand stretched out in sympathy. 'What is the matter, master?'

'I am disappointed, Axata. Bitterly disappointed. I thought you a brother to me. A brother in the eyes of the Powers.'

The convert betrayed a mix of emotions at this declaration – delight at the thought of being so highly regarded, swiftly replaced by alarm that such status seemed to be on the verge of withdrawal. Kor Phaeron continued before Axata had a chance to say anything in response.

'I have placed my trust in you, Axata. Great trust. You are my eyes where I cannot see, my ears where I cannot listen, my tongue where I cannot speak.' These last statements were a direct quote from the famous speech of Tezen in the *Book of Changes,* when the prophet first conjured the duplicitous elemental K'Kaio. Axata trembled, knowing well the verses being thrown at him, and their lesson to be wary of treachery from all others. Kor Phaeron added the final phrase, laden with scorn. 'My hand where I cannot reach, Axata.'

'All is in order, I swear, master,' replied the convert, proffering the notes of lading as though they were the original parables of the prophets. 'I would never d–'

'Do you place your judgement over mine?' snapped Kor Phaeron, turning to generalities to harden his argument before he raised specific accusation.

'N-no, master.'

'Do you think that mortals should second guess the justice of the Powers?'

'Of course not, master. Why...?'

1 8 3

The preacher fixed Axata with a piercing glare, daring him to confess his sins. He let the silence continue, marshalling his ire, directing it until he could no longer contain his righteousness.

'The boy!' Kor Phaeron dropped his voice to a harsh whisper, though he felt like screaming from the masthead. There would be those listening, or trying to, and he would not have them eavesdrop on this exchange. 'I ordered him lashed last night, yet there is not a mark upon his body. It is not your place to spare Lorgar his due punishment.'

'Nor did I, I swear,' said Axata, face flushing. Not with anger but shame. His meaty fists closed around the bills, crumpling the transparencies. 'I put the whip upon him as hard as any of the others.'

Kor Phaeron thought himself a good judge of people, at least in respect to reading their truths and falsehoods. Doing so had provided him with many a lever to extract support or patronage in the time since his exile had begun. In Axata he had a true convert, one who believed in the Truth to his heart. He feared the wrath of the Powers and accepted Kor Phaeron's position as the Bearer of the Word. He could no more lie before his master than he could cut out his own heart and keep living.

'Then we have a different problem, Axata,' Kor Phaeron answered swiftly, changing tack and tone. 'Come with me.'

Axata said nothing as he followed Kor Phaeron along the companionway and up the steps to the main deck. The whole caravan was already moving away from Ad Drazonti, the guard houses hidden behind the surrounding dunes. The priest called for Lorgar to come up from the hold.

The boy responded quickly, casting a nervous glance between the priest and the convert, sensing something was amiss.

'Strip, child,' Kor Phaeron told him.

Lorgar complied after a moment, the pause one of confusion rather than defiance. He pulled off his grey robes to reveal sun-reddened skin over knotted and thick muscle. Clad only in his loincloth he cast the acolyte robe to the deck and stood trembling slightly before Kor Phaeron's sneering scrutiny.

'Turn around,' the preacher said, twirling a finger to emphasise his command. He turned his head to Axata as Lorgar spun on his heel, revealing not even a bruise upon his hard flesh. 'See?'

Axata's surprise was the last confirmation Kor Phaeron needed that the convert was not complicit in some scheme to spare the boy his lashes. With that being the case, there was no further worry of conspiracy and the preacher turned his thought to a fresh concern.

'It seems your whip is not deterrent enough,' Kor Phaeron said aloud for all to hear. 'Gather your five strongest – have them bring their mauls.'

184

Nairo watched with growing horror as Axata stalked about the deck, calling names and giving orders until he and five others waited with thick cudgels in hand. Lorgar stared at them impassively, moving his gaze from one to the next. No one was able to meet his stare for more than a heartbeat before turning their eyes away. Axata was smart enough to not even match gaze with the child, his own fixed upon his master's intent stare.

'You know what needs to be done,' the priest said as he jabbed a finger at Lorgar. 'The body must be scourged for the soul to know purity also.'

'Avoid the head,' Axata muttered to his companions as they surrounded Lorgar with weapons raised, looking to Kor Phaeron for... For what, Nairo wondered? For him to change his mind?

'Do it, or you will feel the touch of chastisement also,' Kor Phaeron said calmly, though Nairo thought he caught for a moment a twitch of consternation at this smallest sign of dissent.

Lorgar raised his fists to his face, elbows touching. Exposing his solid flanks and shoulders, silently accepting the punishment to come.

Axata landed the first blow, on the thigh, and once this was done it was as though a hex was broken and the others joined in, laying their mauls upon Lorgar two-handed. They beat him about the shoulders and ribs, until a blow to the back of the knee sent him sprawling to the deck, where they continued with on his back and legs, working methodically along spine and limbs.

Kor Phaeron gave no order to stop but the men started to tire, their blows lacking force. It was Axata that made the decision, stepping back, dropping his club to the deck from aching fingers. The others retreated, suddenly grateful for the cessation of violence. The withdrawal revealed Lorgar knelt with arms tucked beneath him, forehead on the deck. Every part of exposed flesh was blackened from bruises, here and there a trickle of blood where the skin had broken.

Kor Phaeron stepped closer, kneeling beside him to listen. Nairo also saw the youth's lips moving and strained to hear the quiet words.

'...and in the sixth summer of the Fasting Years, Sennata Tal was thrown into the serpent's cage, and his accusers amongst the unbelievers jeered, and they cursed his name...'

It was from the *Revelations of the Prophets,* the cornerstone of the Covenant's faith. Nairo saw Kor Phaeron watch Lorgar's thick tears drip to the deck before he stood up. He gave a nod to Nairo, who quickly passed the word to others.

He led a cluster of slaves to the child and helped him up. With their assistance, Lorgar hobbled across to the open hatchway, head bowed, back bent. He stopped at the top of the steps and turned his head to Kor Phaeron, one eye blackened where a blow had gone astray. He nodded, as though grateful for the beating. It sickened Nairo to think that Lorgar believed he deserved such a terrible punishment, though he drew hope from what he had seen of the youth's recuperative abilities. Like the whip, the cudgels would leave no lasting injury upon him, and for that Nairo was thankful to the Powers even as he was reminded of the sting across his own back from Axata's attentions the Coldfall before.

Dignity emanated from the boy and Kor Phaeron turned his back on the acolyte, a little too quickly to be purely dismissive, Nairo thought. The preacher picked up the youth's robe and threw it to Nairo without looking at Lorgar.

'Such shall be Lorgar's punishment from now on,' he announced. 'It is only in the Powers' purview to forgive our trespasses, not mine. The sins of the soul will be purged in the flesh.'

1 9 1

From Ad Drazonti the caravan headed into the pitiless expanse known in Vharadesh as the Low Barrens, and to the nomads as The Sands that Slay. Its reputation was well-founded – a four thousand-kilometre sink of pressure and heat and scouring winds that was virtually impassable for three quarters of the year. The oldest myths from the Age Before told of hidden cities and a fall of stars that had created the terrible wilderness. Beasts roamed abroad, that was certain, and beneath the sands even more terrifying apparitions and denizens awaited the bold or foolish.

None were held in more awe than the Kingwyrm: an embodiment of destruction many living within The Sands that Slay worshipped as a demigod, an incarnation of the Powers. The spawn of the Kingwyrm had spread far and wide through the Low Barrens, preying on the unwary and desperate that strayed into the territories.

Tradition held that none passed into the Low Barrens after the Feast of Lamentation, yet it had been three days since that observance and still Kor Phaeron, determined to avoid the slightest contact with any others that might relay the secret of Lorgar to the cities, pressed his caravan along the remains of the old highways into the continent-spanning desolation.

None dared voice their dismay, for to raise complaint against the messenger of the Powers in such a terrible place was to invite disaster. Sacrifices and prayers were conducted with greater zeal than at any previous time in Kor Phaeron's exile, with preacher, acolyte, converts and slaves all bending both their will and their faith to surviving the trials the elements threw against them.

And it seemed as though such dedication was rewarded. For wake-rise after wake-rise, rest-eve after rest-eve, the storms held abated, as though allowing the followers of Kor Phaeron to progress. Even the weathered desert-veterans amongst Axata's warriors, those from the Declined tribes of the Inner Ranges, remarked at this incredible progress. Surely it was a mark of their master's favour in the eyes of the Powers that his people traversed the worst of Colchis' wilds unmolested.

Still they did not take their duties lightly and so it was that when on a terrible Mornday the tempests finally fell upon the sands and engulfed the temple-rig and its escorts, the crews and slaves were well prepared. Sand-shields and windbreaks were erected swiftly. Knowing that any desultory response could prove fatal for them all, Kor Phaeron relented in his prohibition to Lorgar not to labour. With the aid of the extraordinary youth the defences were erected in half the time of any previous attempt. Kor Phaeron joined the work gangs in person, pulling at cables and lifting beams with the others, in what seemed a selfless act for the group.

1 9 2

Nairo was not so convinced of the master's altruism and after all was made ready and the congregation assembled below decks and under their storm shelters, he confided his worries to Lorgar.

'He sees how easy you are with others and is jealous,' Nairo told the boy when they settled below for the wake-main break, when the heat was at its most vicious and even one's soul was scorched despite the shade above. He knew he had to speak carefully, for as much as Lorgar was comfortable among the converts and slaves he was still the acolyte of the master. To speak of Kor Phaeron's tyranny, to lament his beliefs directly would be to speak against the Word and the Truth – concepts in which Lorgar was fully invested despite his suffering under those convictions. 'He worries that you are too popular and tries to usurp some of your manner to himself. He saw how we regarded you when you worked alongside us and stoops to emulate your labours.'

'I would think you had a point,' replied Lorgar, only the glint of his eyes visible in the dark confines of the below deck, 'if you had argued that he laboured for self-preservation.'

'I do, but not against the storms,' said Nairo. He caught the sharp intake of breath from Lorgar and thought he had perhaps dared too much. He took a subtler route to his point than he had intended. 'I remember, "The works of the acolyte lift up the master," so it is said in the *Revelations*.'

'A rejoinder to the accusation that Narag adorned her own reputation with the efforts of Dia Marda and Callipa, meaning that it is to the credit of the master that a pupil achieves high renown.' Nairo could feel the satisfaction emanating from Lorgar. Not smugness, simply a gladness that radiated whenever the youth engaged in theological and scriptural debate. 'Kor Phaeron's elevation by my efforts in no way diminishes my achievements.'

'If he builds upon them as a foundation, you are right,' countered Nairo. He licked his lips. Even in the depths of the temple-rig the dust and grains penetrated, and all was coated with a fine layer of red and grey. 'If he seeks to name your tower as his home, it is a theft. All people should own what they create, to their credit or downfall equally.'

Lorgar did not reply at first and Nairo took heart that the acolyte was turning proper thought upon the subject rather than reeling off some trite counterpoint from the texts. He could feel the boy shift his bulk. He had grown almost as tall as the slave, his rapid growth showing no sign of abating. The meagre rations afforded to even a convert were no match for an appetite that could fuel such development, and Kor Phaeron had demanded that the crew and slaves give up a portion of their own meals to supplement the boy's allotment.

It was a testament to Lorgar's character that such donations were given without resentment, even if it left many hungry. In truth, the slaves had already been on such short rations that they had managed their meals, ensuring that none among their number went too hungry and that each had equal time without.

1 9 3

'Am I not a creation of Kor Phaeron?' Lorgar said eventually. With his growing size his voice had deepened and become richer, and it was clear he was passing through his adolescence even though twenty days earlier he had been no more than an infant. 'His wisdom, zeal and teachings have made me.'

'It is equally a crime to attribute to a mortal that which has been rendered by the Powers,' Nairo stated firmly, pleased to be able to quote Kor Phaeron's doctrines against the master's good. 'You have unique gifts, we all know this. The Powers instilled in you some fate greater than that of any mortal. Many will try to turn you into their tool, for their own ends, but you must stay true to the Will of the Powers. In that, only you can be the arbiter of the Truth.'

Lorgar's reply was softly spoken but even in his quiet tone there was hidden a barb of interrogation.

'And what would the end be, Nairo, to which you would turn me?'

The slave felt stripped bare by the question, any accusation unspoken but no less penetrating for it. Such was the irrepressible nature of Lorgar that he could not avoid the question, nor lie in answer to it.

'I would have all men and women on Colchis be free, Lorgar,' he said, the words dragged forth from his lips. He quickly added, 'If the Powers desire it.'

For what seemed an eternity Lorgar did not reply, and had it not been for his slow breathing Nairo would have thought the youth had slipped away. It made the slave flinch when finally Lorgar laid a broad hand on his leg and spoke.

'I hear you,' he said simply. 'We shall learn if the Powers hear you also.'

And from this Nairo took comfort, until he later thought about the words some more; then he did not, for in his mind only a fool willingly drew the attention of the Powers.

1 10 1

The journey across the Low Barrens became a toil for all, a struggle against an increasingly fierce environment. A few of the smaller vehicles could not withstand the sand-gales and were swallowed or destroyed, several others abandoned or pulled apart for spares, their precious materials and tech reclaimed for future use.

Kor Phaeron pushed them on, extracting every last effort from his followers. He reminded them of the sacrifices of the prophets to bring the Word of the Powers to the cities of Colchis Past.

Survival depended upon their continued crawl across the desert, for if they remained in the heart of the Low Barrens too long they would be swallowed entire by the coming hurricane known as the Godrage, which legend told swept the innermost desert every winter. Each wake-main they had to make progress or suffer even more delays, and so through the fiercest winds, through the skin-shredding tempests and the furnace heat they continued. Like Kap Baha in the *Parable of the Skywhale,* Kor Phaeron was a man possessed, though rather than vengeance he pursued a purer goal – righteous wisdom.

And through such perseverance and the protection of the

Powers, there came a time when the storms abated and Kor Phaeron looked out onto the white peaks of the Razors. Beyond the treacherous passes of the mountains lay the dead city known as the Last Haven, *Sarragen* in the tongue of its long-dead people. Kor Phaeron had not confided the nature of their destination to others, for Sarragen above all the ancient cities was ill-fated in the legends and folklore of the deserts, save for the menace of the Kingwyrm. None returned, it was claimed, and the ghosts of the damned roamed the streets and broken palaces.

Yet to here Kor Phaeron felt drawn. Though he had not been able to make astral observations through the Low Barrens, he was confident that the omens he had seen before had pointed to his destiny being fulfilled in the Last Haven.

Heartened by their victory over the Godrage, the caravan hurried onwards over the plains – a desolation as arid as any on the Periphery but placid and fruitful in comparison to the latter days of their journey.

1 10 2

More and more the converts and slaves looked to Lorgar, if not for leadership, then for physical assistance. Kor Phaeron had allowed his ward to help through the storms and it was now impossible to revoke that permission, even though they had entered tamer climes. Though only half a Colchisian year had passed since Kor Phaeron had plucked Lorgar from the savage Declined, the boy might have been more rightfully called a man, at least in physique. He stood as tall as the preacher and far broader, a match for the burliest guards save for Axata, who towered over all others.

Yet in mind he was not yet mature, despite his evidently

colossal intellect, faultless memory and unprecedented language skills. In matters of emotion and reasoning he was still an innocent in many ways, isolated from the experiences and relationships that would have shaped a normal child of the cities or the desert.

He was singularly Kor Phaeron's charge, placed into his care by the Powers. Despite this great responsibility, and the knowledge that he performed a sacred duty, the preacher found himself looking on the youth as more than just an acolyte. Against all effort to remain aloof and scholarly, a teacher not a parent, Kor Phaeron could not restrain the growing paternal instincts that Lorgar aroused in him.

Knowing that he could not allow any familial bond to distract him from the proper education of Lorgar, Kor Phaeron dedicated himself afresh to instilling the virtues of the Word and the Truth into his adopted son. Every moment Lorgar was not needed seeing to the working and safety of the temple-rig, or catching a brief sleep, Kor Phaeron filled with lessons.

Yet even this was not enough to sate Lorgar's thirst for knowledge, nor remove the seemingly persistent crease of a forthcoming question from his forehead.

1 10 3

'Let me read the books, my master,' Lorgar pleaded one rest-eve after prayers, when the two of them had retired to Kor Phaeron's chambers for the customary study of the *Book of Kairad*, their current occupation. The wind howled outside the shuttered window, scouring paint from the hull with rattles of grit and sand.

'Is not my reading to your liking?' retorted Kor Phaeron. 'Has the sound of my voice become so tiresome?'

'Not these books, my master,' said Lorgar. He pointed to the shelf where Kor Phaeron kept the oldest volumes and those from the most distant cities. Written in foreign and ancient tongues, their titles were a mystery to the preacher, even more so their contents. He had spent much time in contemplation of the illumination, diagrams and illustrations, marvelling at the indecipherable runes and strange figures depicted, but could make no more sense of them than he could the bone-tossing of a Declined soothsayer.

'Those books. The ones you cannot read.'

'You think to pluck their meaning from the Empyrean itself?' said Kor Phaeron scornfully.

'I would like to try to read them.' Lorgar leaned forwards in earnest petition and laid a hand on Kor Phaeron's knee. 'Please... Father?'

The word struck Kor Phaeron like a thunderbolt, sending a shock of equal revelation and revulsion through his body. For an instant the uttering of that title filled him with such profound pride and pleasure that he was giddy with the thought of it. That his feelings for Lorgar were reciprocated, that the child deemed him more than simply an instructor was a vindication and affirmation that Kor Phaeron had never felt before.

Then the reality of the statement turned that joy to bitterness. He slapped away Lorgar's hand and stood up, a heat of embarrassment that turned to anger flushing through him. Kor Phaeron could not look at Lorgar, wrathful and ashamed at the same time.

'Do not use that term again! In all things I am your master, Lorgar, while you are my acolyte.' The circumstance of this change in attitude struck Kor Phaeron as particularly manipulative. The preacher's resentment bested his shame and he turned on Lorgar with damning words flowing unbidden from his lips. 'You think that I would give in to such flattery? That I would allow a son liberties I would not extend to a pupil?'

'No.' Lorgar looked fearfully at the priest, hands held up in supplication. 'I meant no ruse by it, my master.'

'A cheap trick, to sway me to fresh lassitude in my discipline! Close confines in these storms have distracted me, and it seems we have both forgotten hard-learnt lessons of the past.' Kor Phaeron strode to the door and wrenched it open to bellow along the companion way. 'Axata, attend me!'

He glared silently at his ward, daring him to make further excuse for his contemptible behaviour.

1 11 1

Kor Phaeron felt his anger dissipating as he waited for the leader of the converts to attend to his call. Though his ire waned, he knew that he could not relent in seeing through his course of action. If Lorgar was to learn anything from the day it would be strength of purpose – that one's words and deeds have consequence for good or ill, but once set upon a course one had to navigate it to the end.

'Equivocation is for cowards, Lorgar,' he told his pupil. 'Never forget that. Your allies will weaken your resolve with their lack of conviction, and your enemies will seek to undermine your purpose. Be inured to such erosion in all that you do.'

'I will remember that, my master,' said Lorgar, with a quiet vehemence that set a flutter of agitation in Kor Phaeron's chest. He ignored the unsettling sensation, glad of the distraction from Lorgar's fierce gaze that came when Axata arrived.

'Fetch your strongest, Axata,' said Kor Phaeron, his meaning well established by previous such demands.

The convert waited at the door, hands clenched. For several heartbeats he did not meet his master's gaze but then looked directly at him, unspoken apology written in his features.

'They are unwilling, master. Reluctant.' He looked at Lorgar and then back to the preacher, the apology turning to pleading. 'They are afraid to raise rod or whip against the boy.'

'Grown men afraid of a child?' Kor Phaeron curled his lip. 'He grows swiftly but do not forget that he is still a child.'

'I would not hurt you, Axata,' Lorgar said quietly, 'nor hold you responsible for doing the Will of the Powers.'

'That is what worries them.' Axata again moved his gaze quickly between the two of them, nervous and fidgeting. 'Perhaps we could speak away from the boy?'

'Say what needs to be said here,' snapped Kor Phaeron, such little patience as he had quickly worn thin by the giant's hesitancy.

Axata gave a slight shake of the head, fearful but also resolute.

'Come with me,' the priest declared, stomping past Axata, beckoning with an imperious finger. 'We shall settle this.'

He stormed along the companionway and down into the converts' quarters rather than up to the deck. Here he found many of them in their berths, some practising their writing and reading, others discussing scripture, a few in thought or prayer.

There was much rousing at the unexpected arrival of the master, and immediately it was obvious they understood the purpose of his visit. The converts gathered in a group, facing Kor Phaeron, as a herd of goats might confront a stalking sand lion. In truth, physically it was a pride of sand lions confronting a solitary goat, though the priest would never admit it out loud.

1 11 2

Some would later say that arrogance ruled Kor Phaeron's heart, but only those who had not known him. He stood in the light of the Powers and knew nothing of cowardice, only righteousness and the need to spread the Truth. That he took this as his sole duty he would argue was not arrogance but a mere admittance of the burden that had been placed upon his shoulders.

So it was that when he looked upon the converts and sensed their imminent rebellion, the thought of them turning from the Word pained him more than any threat to his well-being.

'You refuse my design,' he said to them, jabbing a finger like a duellist's blade. He named many of them in turn, fierce eyes catching them like the rays of the sun, searing in their intensity. 'Boparus, Kor Alladin, Nomas, Fadau... You, Kaitha? You would deny me?'

Axata intervened, speaking where the others were struck dumb.

'He – Lorgar – is a child of the Powers, master. We all see it, you have spoken of it. He has been sent to us from the Empyrean. The converts have...' He took a breath and straightened, committed to their shared argument. '*We* have decided we will not strike one who has been chosen by the Powers. It will damn us, master, we are sure of it. Our souls – we will not risk our souls by beating him again.'

Fury boiled up inside Kor Phaeron, the insolence and assumption of the converts like sparks on tinder. He mastered the rage, enough to form words through gritted teeth.

'I am the Bearer of the Word, I speak the Truth from the Powers. The Powers act through me, Axata!' He could contain it no more and let the flood of his righteous ire break free. 'Have you read the books? Have you studied the stars and the signs? Ignorant fool! I am the master, the teacher, the Bearer of the Word! I am the Lore and the Law! If you are not fit to enact my command then another will be found. I demand the hands of the next man or woman to refuse me!'

'Then that will be mine,' said Axata, offering his wrists as though Kor Phaeron would sever them there and then. There was no confrontation in his tone, and his manner remained polite and formal. 'Master, we have spoken on this and there is not one among us who will raise a hand against the boy. We ask that you consult with the Powers, master, and seek another way.'

Faced with this naked opposition, Kor Phaeron retained enough presence of mind to realise that he hurtled towards a precipice. In the edge of the Low Barrens he could not countenance a mutiny amongst his caravan, yet his authority had been challenged, his position tarnished.

His mind raced as he sought the means to concede to the fears of the converts whilst retaining mastery of his crew and slaves.

1 11 3

Hearing raised voices, Nairo was drawn to the bulkhead between the slaves' quarters and the more spacious dorms of the converts. He put his ear to the metal, breath still as he listened to the ongoing exchange.

'What's happening?' asked Parentha, creeping up beside him.

'Something about Lorgar. Hush, I'm listening.'

Though he could only hear two words out of every three, it was obvious that the argument was not turning in Kor Phaeron's favour.

'Times are changing,' he told the small group that gathered close by. 'Axata is saying that he will not serve a man who does not acknowledge Lorgar as a new prophet.'

This elicited gasps and exclamations from the nearby slaves. Such a declaration was unheard of – it went against the very founding of the Covenant and the beliefs of Kor Phaeron.

'He'll not agree,' said L'sai. In the gloom of the slave quarters his ebon-skinned companion was barely visible. She cracked her knuckles in agitation, perhaps anticipation, and licked her lips.

'Let's hope he doesn't,' said Nairo. He drew a finger across his throat as though it were a dagger. 'Perhaps Axata will finally do what we have all craved.'

'The converts are as bad as Kor Phaeron,' muttered Parentha. 'You've said that a hundred times.'

'But Lorgar is not,' Nairo assured them. 'If Axata were to swear his loyalty to the boy… Perhaps…'

'You think–' Aladas' protest was cut short by Nairo raising a silencing finger with a glare and a shocked expression.

'Axata just declared that the Powers sent Lorgar to replace Kor Phaeron, that the master has fulfilled his role in finding Lorgar.'

'They'll do it,' whispered L'sai, baring her teeth in a grin. 'Kor Phaeron is too arrogant to step back. He'll have to be cast out.'

'Or more,' suggested Koa No, his enthusiasm for the idea raising the pitch of his voice.

'They've grabbed him!' announced Nairo, hearing angry shouts and the rush of feet. 'They're going to take him on deck!'

The hold suddenly erupted in movement as though filled with swarming rats, as the slaves headed towards the steps below the hatch. Nairo pushed his way to the front, blinking in the sunshine that lit a cloud of dust from above.

Suddenly a hush rippled out through the crowd as a large figure emerged from the shadows, violet eyes catching the shaft of sun through the opening above. He moved quickly, silently. Nairo shrank back from Lorgar as the youth set a foot upon the steps, head bowed under the beams.

'Wait here,' Lorgar told them, face impassive. The words rooted Nairo to the spot, demanding instant compliance though softly spoken.

The acolyte ascended and Nairo watched him go. Only when

Lorgar was out of sight was the slave free to move again and he followed cautiously, skulking up the steps a short distance behind, to peek over the edge of the hatchway.

1 11 4

Trembling with equal fear and excitement, Nairo saw that a handful of the converts had Kor Phaeron in their grasp, while two others were fashioning a noose from cable brought up from below. They had armed themselves from the weapons store – as well as mauls and whips, they carried an assortment of fusils, pistols, bows and blades.

'Exile, I said.' Axata stood a little apart from most, a dozen converts at his back. 'The Powers will decide if he lives or dies.'

'I'll not risk this serpent lying in wait in the sands,' spat back Torsja, her fingers continuing to knot the thick red wire. The Cthollian pulled down her porcelain mask, hiding her expression behind a painted visage of a scowling bat-like apparition. Her voice was muted as she continued, 'We'll send him to the Powers and if they don't want him they can send him back.'

'You will burn for eternity for this heresy!' roared Kor Phaeron. He wrestled an arm free and thrust his hand into the air. 'This night the Powers shall strike you down for laying hands upon the Bearer of the Word. It is not for mortals to defame the flesh of the chosen!'

'You were thrown out of the Covenant for your mad schemes, Kor Phaeron,' laughed Ahengi, one of those holding the preacher. 'Do you not always say that nothing passes but for that within the design of the Powers? If the Powers deign that your unworthy existence should continue, why have they not intervened? We stand beneath their gaze, but where is their hand? What saviour will they send you?'

'They have sent me.'

All eyes turned at Lorgar's quiet pronouncement. Many of the converts shuffled uncomfortably, several brought up their weapons. Axata stepped forwards, hands raised, one to Lorgar and the other to the rest of the converts as though holding back two pugilists.

Others had come aboard, bringing their vehicles in either at some prearranged signal or simply noticing that all was not well on the temple-rig. The deck was becoming quite crowded and Nairo could see other slaves peering up through the gratings and from the companionway stair beyond the confrontation.

'Let us not do anything hasty, brethren and sistren,' the chief convert said forcefully. 'Lorgar, this is for the best. Kor Phaeron has been poisoning your mind.'

'Unhand my father.' Lorgar took a step, and there was nothing aggressive in his demeanour, but the converts retreated from him as though he pushed them back with his presence.

'Your father?' Torsja grabbed hold of Kor Phaeron and forced the noose over his shaven head. 'If you have a father, we left his corpse in that mongrel nomad camp.'

'Leave him be,' insisted Lorgar, taking another step.

'Do as he says,' said Axata, turning fully towards the other converts. 'As we agreed, we shall send him into the desert to seek his fate.'

'You will not,' said Lorgar. 'You will take your hands from the Bearer of the Word.'

'Do as he says.' Axata recoiled from Lorgar as the youth approached, as if pained by the youngster's presence. 'We will find another way. The prophet has spoken.'

'He is no prophet,' snarled Ahengi, the white tattoos on his dark flesh twisting in grotesque curls as he bared sharpened teeth. 'Look at him – he is an abomination. A sand-born mutant. The Powers have cursed him, not gifted him.'

Witnessing this, Nairo realised how divisive Lorgar's presence had become. To each member of the caravan he was now a powerful symbol, but none were agreed on what he represented. The hatred on Ahengi's face, repeated on others, betrayed a counter-cult within the converts, fuelled not by Kor Phaeron or Axata, but the jealous words of Ahengi.

'We must cast out those who would bring the curses of the Powers upon us,' the would-be demagogue continued. Axata shook his head in disbelief, confused by the subversion of his own play for power. Where moments before there had been Kor Phaeron against a single faction, now the converts split into smaller groups as other allegiances and agendas were revealed.

The priest's expression was unreadable, a complex and changing mix of anger, fear, loathing and surprise at each new development. The edifice of his power had fallen apart in just moments, though the foundations had slowly been eroding from the moment he had brought Lorgar into his congregation.

'Slay the body and release the tainted soul – it is the only way to save ourselves,' declared Torsja, yanking on the noose about Kor Phaeron's neck.

'If you insist,' said Lorgar, bunching his long fingers into fists.

1 11 5

When later asked to describe those following moments, Nairo was at a loss to relate them. His first response was one of despair, that the creed of Kor Phaeron had been so inculcated into Lorgar's mind that he would save the preacher from his just demise at the hands of those he had consistently bullied and degraded. In that instant Nairo thought all his hopes for Lorgar were rendered broken, scattered to the winds like the ashes of the nomad camp in which the boy had been found.

This despair became horror quite swiftly, at the thought that Lorgar would give up his life in that unworthy cause. As fusils hummed into life and feyblades crackled, the old slave was certain that Ahengi and his companions would execute the son as they would the father.

After that, the incident became a blur. Nairo would later recall the snap of gunfire and the hiss of arrows, the shouts of anger that soon became cries of agony and panic. Where Lorgar had been was empty air, and where the converts had stood became a stack of broken bodies, bones snapped, limbs wrenched from their sockets, organs torn bloodily from the carcasses.

In just half a dozen heartbeats Lorgar stood among the ruin of his work, the blood of Torsja and several others spattered across his acolyte robe and face. His hands dripped with crimson, the blood pooling on the metal deck at his feet.

Kor Phaeron stood with mouth agape at the carnage, in the centre of mangled corpses with Lorgar by his side.

Nairo wept, the sudden violence more grotesque than anything he had seen before. He saw tears in the eyes of Kor Phaeron also, a distinct memory of them glittering in the light of a fallen feyblade, for the sun that burned bright above was shrouded by the shade of the awnings. Yet there was triumph in the eyes of the preacher too, a pride in his gaze as he looked upon the death wrought by his acolyte.

The whine of a fusil shot broke the scene, hitting Lorgar in the shoulder. The youth went down to one knee, flesh burning with the gleam of the energy impact. Seeing that the chosen of the Powers still lived despite this wound, Ahengi and the others fled, firing wild shots with their pistols and fusils to cover their flight into the sands.

1 12 1

The stench of blood and charred flesh was strong in Kor Phaeron's nostrils. The bulk of Lorgar close at hand was dominating but reassuring, the drip of fluid from his fingers a faint drumbeat on the deck.

'My son…' whispered the priest, overcome with emotion. He placed his splayed fingers upon the wound in Lorgar's shoulder, but the youth did not flinch from the touch. Already the tissue was healing, the raw edges of the cauterisation softening into fresh muscle and skin.

'It will pass, my master.' Lorgar turned his gaze over the rail, to the cloud of dust that marked the passage of the mutineers. 'We are well rid of them.'

Kor Phaeron's heart hardened again.

'Foolish Lorgar,' he said. 'Torsja was correct – one does not leave an enemy to recover. When one strikes, one must do so to the fullest extent of power, to leave no foe remaining that might challenge the victor.'

'They will not return,' Lorgar replied. 'No water, no food. The sunwolves will be picking their bones within days.'

Kor Phaeron chose not to admonish Lorgar for omitting

his title, judging the moment too precarious to waste on such trivialities. As always, his view was from a loftier position, seeing further than those around him. The only thing he believed in more than the Word and the Truth was the persistence of enemies.

'It takes only one to bring word of your existence to Vharadesh,' he explained slowly, as though Lorgar were an infant again. His ward thought too well of people and circumstance; it left him vulnerable to the vicissitudes of the Powers' arcane plans and the petty ambitions of mortals who would deny that design. Kor Phaeron wafted a hand towards the dead traitors around them. 'If any doubted your origins in the Empyrean before this day, none do so now. All will desire to court you or destroy you if they hear of what you can do.'

He grabbed Lorgar's bloodied hand in his fingers, clutching it tightly, earnestly. Kor Phaeron did not fear death or indignation or any of the petty tremors in other men's hearts – righteousness put right any dread of such mortal concerns – but he was not carved from rock.

'You have been led to me, son, and I to you. The Powers have willed this to be, and thus shall it be. But there are those who would not have it so, who would allow their vanity to overturn the Will of the Powers. The Covenant is the strongest church of Colchis and by whatever means, they will learn of you, Lorgar. If just one of those faithless dogs brings word to another, as the cold of the night follows the heat of the day we can be sure that tribe by tribe, trader by trader, city by city, the news of your being shall reach Vharadesh. And when it does, the despots of that city, the tyrants who chain the Faithful to the drudgery of recitations and empty ceremony, will see you dead. Or worse, your glory bent beneath the yoke of their empty worship, for they will suffer no other, not even the Powers, to eclipse them in praise.'

As was his way, Kor Phaeron did not have to specify his desire, for it was plain from circumstance what needed to be done. Through him the Truth was known even though he did not have to give voice to the Word.

1 12 2

'Say no,' whispered Nairo, barely breathing the words, remembering the keen hearing of Lorgar.

The boy made no indication that he had heard the slave, and for a moment did not respond to the emotional petition of Kor Phaeron.

'I will come,' said Axata, bending a knee to the master and acolyte. 'To atone for the mistake, and the peril I unleashed upon this blessed congregation.'

The offer was repeated by the guards who had remained with the leader of the converts, and they bowed to the deck before Lorgar.

'No.' The youth spoke but one word, giving no further argument – yet it was absolute, as final as the sound of a tomb lid falling into place. He started towards the side of the deck, heading for the ladder.

'They will be prepared this time,' Axata warned, rising.

'Perhaps,' said Lorgar, not looking back.

'They have weapons.' Axata proffered his pistol to the youth. 'You should take something too.'

Lorgar considered this, looking at the gun.

'Weapons are a falsehood, giving the weak the illusion that they are strong.' He smiled at Axata, and it seemed as though the sun penetrated the shade for a heartbeat. 'But I take your point.'

Lorgar paced the deck, looking around the temple-rig. In the aft section had been stored the remains of several of the vehicles broken apart during the crossing of the Low Barrens. The youth rifled through the parts for a short while and then turned, the axle of a cart in one hand, the heavy head of a mast-censer in the other. He pushed the spiked iron globe onto the shaft, his fingers bending the metal into place.

In one hand he raised the mace, a weapon heavier than anything Axata could have carried.

'Wait for me here,' said Lorgar, and there was no arguing with his command, even from Kor Phaeron, whose nature made him oppose on instinct any who tried to instruct him.

'Stay safe,' said Nairo, the sentiment echoed by a few other slaves as the youth climbed onto the ladder.

His last glance was for Kor Phaeron. The priest returned the look with customary indifference.

'Make me proud, child,' said the preacher. 'Spare none.'

And with that Lorgar descended. Nairo, Axata and many others crowded the rail, watching the boy stride across the sands. Kor Phaeron gave a contemptuous snort and headed to his cabin.

'It is in the hands of the Powers now,' he declared before descending below deck.

The slaves and remaining converts stayed watching until long after Lorgar had been swallowed by the haze of distance and the wind had erased his footprints.

1 12 3

Following Lorgar's departure a strange mood fell upon the caravan. Kor Phaeron did not emerge from isolation, occasionally shouting demands for fresh water and food, but communicating no more than that. The slaves performed such duties as necessary for the bare minimum requirements of hygiene and sustenance. The guards – barely a quarter of their number remained – were reluctant to enforce any further labour upon those below them, now outnumbered a further threefold by the departure of the mutineers.

There remained a possibility that the heretics who had turned away from the Truth might return, but to patrol and post sentries would leave the converts with barely a handful of warriors to act as wardens on the temple-rig.

Some of the slaves, L'sai acting as spokesperson, demanded that they be armed from the lockers, arguing that the converts who remained would be no match for those who had been chased away. To the converts this was not only a practical nightmare, but also an injunction against all they had been taught by Kor Phaeron.

Axata and Nairo came to a quick arrangement that the guards would not administer any punishments whilst the slaves would make no attempt to harm either the converts or Kor Phaeron. Neither group could exist without the other for the time being, nor was willing to challenge the quickly established status quo.

To cement this agreement the two factions prayed together, asking the Powers for guidance and protection and strength in the trying times. They cursed the mutineers as faithless and implored the Powers to strike down those who had turned from the Truth.

1 12 4

The wake-main of Long Noon passed without incident, and rest-eve. Wake-rise came without sight or sound of Lorgar or the mutineers returning. Kor Phaeron did not emerge from his prayers, studies or whatever activity kept him in his quarters, which suited both the converts and the slaves well. The truce that had been established continued through three more meals and prayer sessions, and endured into Duskeve also.

At the crest of wake-main on Duskeve, as twilight hastened towards Coldfall, Axata approached Nairo.

'I have a fear,' he confessed to the old slave. 'The deniers had little time gained on Lorgar before he left. It would not have taken this long for him to catch up with them.'

'I agree. He would outpace them and his endurance is endless,' said Nairo. 'He would have returned by now if he could.'

'We must accept that he is lost to us.' Axata's dark eyes glittered with moisture at the thought, and the declaration caught Nairo's breath in his throat and constricted about his heart. 'Lorgar has become a martyr. Too young, he has been taken from us.'

'I'll not give up hope,' Nairo argued, fighting back the sadness that had seeped into his soul. 'He might have prevailed and now, injured, lies waiting for us in the sands.'

'It is no comfort that he will die a slow death instead,' moaned Axata.

'You misunderstand. We should send out a party to search for Lorgar.'

'Such a group would have to be armed,' Axata replied, eyes narrowing with suspicion. 'If converts leave, the caravan would be defenceless if the mutineers return. Unless you think I would arm the slaves. Is that your intent?'

'Perhaps it is time that we show a little faith?'

'That the Powers protect Lorgar?'

'I do not doubt that, but that wasn't my meaning. We should show faith in each other.'

'I can't, Nairo. The master's mood is as unpredictable as ever. The Powers move him in strange ways and can you tell me what he is thinking now, after everything that has just happened?'

'No,' admitted Nairo. 'This treachery – your treachery – could send him beyond the edge of reason.'

'A precipice we can both agree he walks along at the best of times.'

Nairo could not ignore this plain fact. If he examined his heart he could not in conscience assure the safety of the priest, from himself or any of the other slaves.

'We must leave it to the Powers,' Axata declared suddenly. 'Their design will come to pass. It is not for mortals to judge.'

'I have always found that fatalistic, Axata,' said Nairo.

'I don't mean that we'll do nothing – quite the opposite. I will take the converts at dawn tomorrow, but I will not arm you in our stead. If the mutineers come back and not us... Well, either we'll already be dead or I promise I'll do my best to avenge you and the master. And if you think to attack Kor Phaeron, know that the wrath of the Powers will be unrelenting in vengeance for the Bearer of their Word.'

Nairo saw that the giant had made up his mind, and thought that perhaps the absence of the guards would provide some opportunity yet to be seen.

He did not tell the others, lest they fell to unnecessary scheming before the converts left, which might reach the ear of Axata.

The rest-eve of Duskeve arrived, bringing its cold touch. Though tired, Nairo slept fitfully, agitated by the prospect of what Coldfall might bring.

1 12 5

He turned the old pages again. Each leaf of the wafer-thin plastek curved without creasing, its sheer surface untouched by the ravages of time. Kor Phaeron ran a dirty finger along the inked lines, marvelling at the fluidity of the script, not seeing the ragged nail chewed to the skin. It was unlike the cuneiform that dominated the modern languages of Colchis, more akin to a flowing river of thought than isolated word-forms. He looked at the beautiful illustrations, full of vibrant colour even centuries, perhaps millennia after they had been crafted. The slender figures who represented the various rituals and prayer positions with their knowing eyes, superbly captured by crystalline threads of miraculous ink.

The book was remarkably light in his hands. It was thin compared to the many weighty volumes that sat on the makeshift shelves, so that it felt as though he held no more than a feather.

Kor Phaeron had often wondered what knowledge lay in the pages of the book, tantalisingly just out of reach. Was the answer he sought right here, hidden behind the words he could not read? Was it part of the Powers' cosmic joke that they had given him the key to the Truth, placed it right before his eyes, but blinded him to its presence?

He cursed his own ineptitude, and cursed again the mania that fuelled his mind. The fervour of faith burned so brightly, so hotly in his soul that it was impossible to resist. It was the fuel to his zeal, but it had a price, and now he had paid that account in terrible dues.

A wavering hand wiped away the sweat from his brow, then moved to the moisture that wet his cheeks.

He had sent away his son, sent him to his death most likely.

More than that, he had deprived the world of the Powers' great gift.

Kor Phaeron hated that the Powers had made him the Bearer of the Word. He thought of the title and laughed, but in bitterness not humour. The appellation had occurred to him in a fevered sleep, ten days into his exile, burning in the desert. The books he had stolen from the temple had been his salvation, the shield against attack, the proof of his identity.

He let the book fall from shivering fingers and he stood up, reaching towards the other indecipherable tomes held on the wall. He pulled out one at random, its leather cover inlaid with the spotted remains of gold leaf, the title as distant from him as the Empyrean itself.

Kor Phaeron threw it on the floor, and grabbed another, and this volume he let fall from numb fingers also. And the others, with sudden craving, he pulled from the chest-shelf, toppling the books about his feet.

The piles of bent pages and cracked spines reminded him of the old etchings, of heretics and martyrs bound to the stake, firewood around them, the flames scorching the sin from their flesh.

He looked at the lantern, reached a trembling hand towards the oil-fuelled light. Forlorn, he gazed down upon the works of the unknown authors and felt all purpose ebb from his body.

1 13 1

Shouts on the deck above dimly penetrated Kor Phaeron's consciousness. He ignored them, as he had ignored all other outside stimulus in his days of isolation. Let the slaves and converts do as they wished; it would be in the lap of the Powers, just as he had set Lorgar free into the wilds to whatever unkind fate awaited him.

The thought of Lorgar doubled his grief, for he had lost not only his faith but the only one who had shown him the truest passion and understanding. Never now would those books be read, for in his pride and vanity he had thrown away the key given to him by the Powers.

He had failed. He had failed his congregation and the Powers, and he had failed their chosen messenger, Lorgar.

There came a furious knocking at the cabin door but he ignored it, stepping to grab the lantern from its hook in the ceiling.

The door rattled and shivered as those outside threw their weight against it.

The slaves, he suspected. Finally the converts had abandoned him and now the slaves would have their vengeance. He would deny them that injustice, for he had been only the vessel.

Against the assault the feeble lock could not hold and the door flew open with a crash, revealing Axata and Nairo, with others clustered into the companionway behind them.

'Master!' The chief convert shouldered aside the wreckage of the door.

'It is all lost, Axata. The Powers have abandoned me.'

'Lorgar lives, my master,' said Nairo, the words reluctantly shared. 'The lookouts have spied him returning. He lives.'

1 13 2

Never before had Nairo seen such fluctuating emotions on a man's face. Kor Phaeron had been the picture of despair when they had broken open the door – a course of action that Axata had insisted upon, for Nairo would have been happy to leave Kor Phaeron to whatever darkness of the soul had taken him. The preacher's grimed face was streaked with the tracks of tears, eyes raw and red. His robes were in disarray, revealing ragged scratch marks on the chest and shoulders where he had clawed at himself. His face was similarly criss-crossed with marks.

Disbelief quickly replaced the grief, and then confusion. For just an instant Nairo saw happiness, unparalleled joy in fact, before Kor Phaeron's demeanour reverted to that which the congregation knew so well. Scorn.

'You speak as if surprised,' snapped the Bearer of the Word. 'Is he not the gift of the Powers? This is vindication, that he has been returned to me. Blessed are we that the Powers turn their gaze upon us.'

Axata and Nairo exchanged a look at this rapid reversal, taken aback by the sudden emergence of the old Kor Phaeron. Nairo thought to mention that the priest seemed similarly on the verge of giving up, but had no opportunity. Kor Phaeron strode towards them, adjusting his robe as he crossed the cabin, forcing Axata to step aside. It was as if nothing had happened, that they had come upon him studying his books and writing his observations as they had done a thousand times before.

'Out of the way,' Kor Phaeron snapped, when Nairo was tardy in moving from the door.

The companionway was narrow and the cluster of converts and slaves was forced to retreat up the steps, spilling onto the illuminated deck like water forced by a pump, with Kor Phaeron advancing implacably after them. Axata emerged a step behind and pointed over the preacher's shoulder, to the figure in the starlit distance.

A wagon had been sent out to fetch him and they could see Lorgar taken on board. They waited in silence as the vehicle turned and headed back towards the temple-rig, thick wheels churning the ceaselessly moving sand.

1 13 3

They crowded the rail as the wagon neared, though a respectful empty space remained around Kor Phaeron. Nairo studied the preacher's expression, seeking some sign of his intent. The Bearer of the Word stared into the distance, following the course of the wagon without reaction. Yet when the vehicle came alongside and Lorgar could be seen, there was the merest hint of something, but it chilled Nairo to see it: triumph.

Nairo could feel his world slipping away again. Kor Phaeron would emerge from the mutiny stronger and more zealous than ever. It mattered not that Axata and his converts were much diminished; with Lorgar returned Kor Phaeron would be all-powerful again. Yet the slave could not resent the youth's survival. He looked down at the wagon and saw the boy, skin darkened by the sun but not reddened or blistered as it should have been after such exposure the unrelenting elements. The sight of Lorgar filled him with joy, an elevation of the spirit beyond the simple pleasure of seeing an ally returned.

With easy movements, Lorgar jumped from the wagon to the ladder up the side of the temple-rig. In one hand he held his mace, its head and shaft dark with dried blood, as was the youth's arm. His chest was splashed with the same, though run through with tributaries of sweat across his golden skin. He hauled himself to the deck and stood before Kor Phaeron, head slightly bowed.

'It is done, my master,' said Lorgar. 'None were spared.'

The converts and slaves lifted their voices in praise and gave wordless cheer to this pronouncement. Kor Phaeron matched the youth's look, fixing him with his gaze. Nairo saw a flicker of something in Lorgar's face, just the smallest of changes. A subtle challenge, perhaps, as he held the priest's stare rather than looking away in deferment. In Kor Phaeron's eye he saw something of recognition too. He gave the slightest of nods and stepped back.

1 13 4

As he did so, Kor Phaeron seemed to notice the book in his hand. Nairo had not paid it any heed, but it seemed the preacher had been holding it when they had broken into his cabin. Now he recognised it, just as Kor Phaeron looked down and saw it also.

The Revelations of the Prophets. The holiest book on Colchis.

Kor Phaeron held it up like a banner, for all on the temple-rig and beyond to see.

'The Powers have made their Will known to me!' he declared.

'The Truth is revealed and their blessings laid upon our cause. Lorgar is returned to us, one of the Faithful, a servant to the Word.'

'A servant, my master? Not a slave?' Had he not been so close, Nairo might have missed Lorgar's whispered question.

The youth looked at Kor Phaeron and then at the book in the preacher's hand, his meaning pointed but lost on the slave. Kor Phaeron seemed to understand the intent and paused in his delivery to spend a heartbeat evaluating Lorgar's stare. The priest nodded, a little reluctantly at first but again with more vehemence while whatever thoughts that uncoiled inside his brain took form. When he spoke it was with slow deliberation, which might have been taken for emphasis but Nairo could see that it was simply a mask for a lingering uncertainty. The priest's gaze did not move from Lorgar even though it seemed his words addressed them all.

'A time of testing, I have said before. All of us must undergo it, be it as master or slave or convert. Or acolyte. Our doubts made manifest, our enemies both real and phantasmal laid before us. The Powers have no need of the weak. They reward the strong. As I was shown the path to the Truth while I wandered the unforgiving sands, so Lorgar has placed himself before their immortal gaze, proving his worth and writing his faith with the blood of our foes.' Kor Phaeron's hesitancy had gone, his voice now strident once more. He thrust the book towards Lorgar, who looked at it with surprise and bafflement for a moment before he took it.

'It has been made clear to me that I tread a different path from now. My present course is run. Though I shall remain your guide in all matters of faith, a new messenger has been delivered to us.' Kor Phaeron smiled at Lorgar and, anticipating what was to come, Lorgar beamed back, his joy infectious. His excitement seeped into Nairo to the delight of the slave, even as the rational part of his mind screamed in despair as Kor Phaeron's grip on the boy took a new and even more dangerous turn.

The priest stepped back and bent one knee before Lorgar, eliciting gasps from the converts and slaves together.

'Behold our new Bearer of the Word!'

AFTER MONARCHIA

963.M30

The Fidelitas Lex, Over Khur

Before he even set foot inside the chamber of his primarch Kor Phaeron could smell the stench of sweat, burned flesh and pungent blood through the swirl of spicy incense. The crack of a flail startled the Keeper of Faith and he stepped swiftly inside.

Lorgar sat cross-legged upon the bare floor, a seven-tailed scourge in one hand. His other lay in his lap, as though in quiet repose. With serpent-quick vehemence the primarch lashed the scourge across his shoulder and back, laying the knotted tails upon his flesh with a drawn-out slap. The blow would have crippled lesser beings but the primarch's only reaction was a twitch of the lip.

Through a layered daub of grey ash his skin was in tatters. A remarkably disturbing achievement given his Emperor-gifted physiology. Testament to the viciousness and persistence of Lorgar's self-flagellation for the last three days.

At his side was a gold-rimmed bowl of white clay – a font from one of the many chapels of the *Fidelitas Lex*. Within the metre-broad dish were ashes and charred remnants. Lorgar noticed the perplexed look of the Keeper of Faith.

'All that is left of proud Monarchia,' the primarch said quietly, his expression haunted. He dipped his hand into the ashen mess and let pieces fall through his fingers. 'Buildings. People. A lifetime of endeavour. My foolish pride.'

'None should be prouder,' declared Kor Phaeron. The door whispered shut behind him. He spied a brazier in the adjoining room, its coals now embers, the heat of it glimmering on the wall where a tapestry of the Emperor had once hung, now torn down to reveal bare wall.

In the brazier he saw several irons, their heads shaped as the various runes of Colchis – sigils Lorgar himself had created to represent the new faith he had ushered in. Signs of the One, of the Truth and the Word.

He saw burn marks upon the flesh of Lorgar, branding fit for a sternback that would have overcome a mortal with pain.

'How...?'

'A servitor of the Mechanicum makes a useful unthinking factotum on occasion. Devoid of conscience, they will happily perform any instruction for days on end. No remorse, no hesitation. An instrument of succour in these dark times.'

It was a delicate moment and Kor Phaeron judged that Lorgar did not need instruction as much as guidance, to be returned to the path he sought. He affected his most fatherly demeanour.

'You asked for me. You wish to talk, my son?'

'And Erebus, though I have allowed us a brief time to converse before he arrives. There is a matter that we must discuss and it is not for his ears. Not yet, I would say.'

'This scourging, it is because of Monarchia,' said Kor Phaeron. 'The crime is not yours.'

'It was and remains so. There is not an accusation levelled against us that we can defend. What we sought to create in purity was a distortion of the Truth. The Emperor cares not for these worlds, save as numbers in a ledger on Terra. We thought we crafted jewels for the Imperial crown, but all we have been doing is wasting our time polishing worthless lumps of earth.'

'Not worthless, for our faith is our meaning, whether the Emperor requires it or not.'

'He does not, and we will comply.' The word brought a twist of disgust to the primarch's lips. 'Compliance. A word that sounds so innocent yet we now know to be so loaded with meaning.'

'We cannot abandon who we are, Urizen.' Kor Phaeron struggled to think how he might lift Lorgar from his malaise. The blow to his beliefs, to his core of being – to his soul, though the Emperor denied such a thing existed – had been catastrophic. As one father had turned the Golden One's works to nought, the other would have to raise him from the ruins of their destruction.

'There is another way,' the Keeper of Faith suggested.

'You saw what happened to Monarchia. My father's judgement is absolute. We must dissolve all accoutrements of our beliefs, become the exterminators He built us to be.'

'This could break our Legion apart,' warned Kor Phaeron. 'Faith holds us together. For many it is what binds them to you, to the Imperium. They follow the prophet of a god, not a warlord of an Emperor.'

'It is not the first time my authority has been tested.'

'It is not.'

'And before there was a Brotherhood of like-minded souls prepared to defend the Truth.'

'There was.' Kor Phaeron knew well to which organisation Lorgar referred – if it could even be called a organisation. A movement, of dedicated followers willing to protect the Faith at all costs.

Was Lorgar really asking Kor Phaeron to do it again? The primarch would never say as much, perhaps could never bring himself to do so. He knew little enough of the Dark Heart and the Brotherhood that had defended the Truth on Colchis.

Kor Phaeron had to be sure; a misstep now, when the Legion's morale and his primarch's conviction were so broken, would prove fatal for the Word Bearer and his position.

'What point in being the Keeper of Faith when there is no faith to keep?' he asked quietly.

'You are my First Captain still,' Lorgar assured him. 'Your rank, our history, cannot be so easily undone. Our bond is stronger even than the foundations of a city.'

'You wish to expunge all evidence of our faith from the Legion?'

'None must espouse the Emperor as a god.'

And there it was, the deceleration that Kor Phaeron needed. Strange and circuitous were the ways of the Powers sometimes, yet one could see the slow flowing of their course from the correct perspective.

How apt that the Powers had clad themselves in the guise of the Emperor Himself, to shield Colchis from His ire. Through Lorgar they had found the means to hide from the gaze of their would-be destroyer, concealing a blade aimed at the heart of the Imperium dedicated to their overthrow.

The Emperor's disregard for Lorgar, His contempt for the great work done in His name, provided opportunity. Kor Phaeron met his adopted son's gaze, holding that violet stare for just a moment, seeking connection.

Moisture glistened there. Lorgar knew full well what he was asking. Did he know truly where the course inevitably would lead? It was Kor Phaeron's role to guide him to that conclusion.

'There will be bloodshed,' said the First Captain, meaning both from Lorgar's request and the demand of the Emperor. The

Powers demand sacrifice, he reminded himself. To each they give position; from each a price to pay. Lorgar's debt would be levied in sorrow. The Lore and the Law. 'A new war, like nothing before.'

'I am no stranger to such an undertaking.'

The chime of the door warden system alerted them to a new arrival.

At Lorgar's command the door hissed open to reveal Erebus, clad in the black robe of a Chaplain. The Word Bearer stopped suddenly at the threshold as he caught sight of his primarch's appearance, a mixture of horror and sorrow etching his weathered features.

'Come in, I would speak with you,' Lorgar bid him before returning to his conversation. 'Do you remember, Kor Phaeron? We called it the Last War. How history makes a vanity of such things.'

'I remember it,' the Keeper of Faith murmured.

BOOK 2: ASCENDANCE

112 years ago [Terran standard]
23.3 years ago [Colchisian calendar]

2 1 1

Kor Phaeron watched from the shadow of the deck, his calculating gaze moving from the crowd gathered in the shade of the temple-rig to Lorgar in the pulpit and back again. Another Declined tribe, held in rapture by the acolyte's words, staring up at him as he delivered another self-written sermon.

When the preacher had first passed the title of Bearer of the Word eight days before, it had been a moment of necessity, desperation almost. Yet he looked back to see in that instant also the hand of the Powers, for it had been an inspired decision. The benefits were many, most obviously that Lorgar commanded far more natural loyalty than Kor Phaeron could have ever hoped for himself. There was not a soul whose path they had crossed who was not moved by his words, not touched by his passion and faith. Though they had been avoiding contact, the number of such souls was gradually swelling the size of the congregation.

Kor Phaeron looked around the camp. It was twice the size it had been before he had met Lorgar, more than replacing the slain converts. Their tents and wagons, their families and beasts made the affairs of the caravan more complicated. However, as they were all theoretically converts, Kor Phaeron had made feeding, organising and dealing with the newcomers the problem of Axata. The responsibility seemed like a boon to the master of converts, whereas in fact it enabled the priest to keep the newcomers out of his affairs.

And such affairs he now had time to ponder and shape and grow as he desired, unfettered by the demands of sermonising and seeing to the soul-being of his congregation. Lorgar was truly the means to salvation, a figurehead like no other. That he took the eyes of the many away from Kor Phaeron was of great value, and as with Axata the role itself seemed to be its own reward. Lorgar had never looked happier as when he stood before a willing audience listening to his stirring speeches – except perhaps when he spoke in private with Kor Phaeron, wrangling over some newly translated nugget of information from the books that Kor Phaeron had finally allowed him to read.

They had arranged one such session for that wake-main and Lorgar took the final prayers of the gathering quickly, eager to meet with his teacher; another slight change in Kor Phaeron's positioning from master, but one that made no substantive difference to the influence he held. In reality, Lorgar was a far better proselytiser of Kor Phaeron's ideas than he had ever been himself. Possessed of fiery disposition upon the pulpit but able to extend empathy and compassion where the priest was hardened to life's miseries and uncaring of others' petty burdens.

The two of them descended to Kor Phaeron's chamber – Lorgar insisted in remaining billeted with the slaves despite his new rank and purpose, but spent most of his time here with the library. It was to the books that the youth now moved, plucking one from the shelf without hesitation to present to Kor Phaeron. His expression was one of eagerness.

'I think I have finished translating this one,' he said. Kor

Phaeron looked at the book. It was the one with the flowing scripts and strange pictures. Lorgar continued, talking at pace. 'It is like nothing else in the library. None of the other languages and dialects came close to helping decode it, so I had to start from scratch. I think, and I know what this sounds like, but I think it is not human in origin.'

Kor Phaeron frowned.

'Not human?'

'The pictures, the references, the entire reality described in the text is nothing like a human experience.' Lorgar's passion faltered and his expression became a lopsided smile. 'The truth is, I think it's either a book of poetry, or a guide to culinary artistry.'

'A guide to...?'

'I know,' Lorgar shrugged. 'It's quite opaque and I might be wrong. I shall keep working on my translation, but I do not think the contents will be shedding any further light upon the Truth.'

2 1 2

Lorgar sat down on the bed, which made the floor creak for he had continued to grow at an outstanding pace and now stood taller even than Axata. His appetite was immense, fuelling his huge body even as the books and Kor Phaeron did the same for his equally massive intellect. The youth sighed.

'You are not content?' Kor Phaeron asked the question lightly, but the last thing he desired was a restless Lorgar. The youth had a tendency to seek out answers for questions others did not even ask. Any sign of ennui signalled work for Kor Phaeron.

'I am not sure of what the Powers intend,' confessed Lorgar. He rested his elbows on his knees and clasped his gigantic hands together. 'There is barely a sentence in all of this library that I have not inscribed upon my thoughts, but I am no closer to seeing the Truth. I Bear the Word as you did, and the converts grow in number, but this cannot be what the Powers desire of us.'

Kor Phaeron said nothing, knowing that it was not the time to make suggestions. Lorgar had a look he now recognised well, of a course of thoughts running on their own lines, not to be disrupted.

'I – we – are missing something, I think. What we seek is not in the books, but in the stars perhaps.'

'You have mastered the arts of the observations and know every single entry in the *Heavenly Scripts* by heart.'

'And nightly we chart the constellations and seek some sign from the Powers of what to do. And what do they say?'

'Nothing,' admitted Kor Phaeron. 'Their gaze is elsewhere, Lorgar. The Powers are infinite beings but they do not waste their attention on the unworthy. The crimes of the Covenant. Their demolition of true faith brought the apathy of the Powers to Colchis.'

'And how will we reignite that faith, my teacher?'

'With hard…' He fell quiet as he noticed a distant, absent look in the youth's eye. As though he stared through the wall. 'Are you listening to me?'

There was no reaction from Lorgar at first. Kor Phaeron resisted the urge to raise his voice, to strike Lorgar from his reverie. He saw the youth's lips moving ever so slightly though the rest of him was immobile.

'What are you saying? Speak up!'

'Listen, father…' Kor Phaeron winced at the use of the patriarchal title. Occasionally Lorgar regressed to such familiarity when he forgot himself. 'Listen to the music.'

Kor Phaeron strained to hear but no music came to his ears, only the usual noises of the temple-rig readying to continue onwards until rest-eve. He moved to the window and opened it, in full knowledge that Lorgar's hearing was uncannily good, like all of his senses and much else about him. Still he did not hear any pluck of a string or pipe of a flute.

'I hear nothing, boy,' he said, but realised that Lorgar's gaze had not shifted from its mesmeric state. He conscious mind was not within the cabin.

2 1 3

All of a sudden Lorgar threw himself backwards onto the cot with a hoarse shout, cracking the timbers beneath his weight. The bed collapsed to the floor with the youth atop. Hands held up to his temples, eyes wide with shock, Lorgar roared, deafeningly loud in the close confines of the chamber. The sound of it toppled Kor Phaeron, sending him crashing to the floor with his hands over his ears, head reeling from the violence of the outburst.

Ringing in his ears, spots in front of his eyes, Kor Phaeron squinted across the cabin floor to see Lorgar rolling from side to side, mouth opening and closing like a landed fish, eyes roaming and roving with wild motion. Still dizzy, Kor Phaeron crawled closer, stretching out a hand to comfort his beleaguered ward. His chest felt tight, his throat knotted at the sight of Lorgar beset by fits and tics.

'Calm, calm,' croaked the priest, panic gripping him as he seized Lorgar's huge hand in both of his own, trying to squeeze hard enough for the touch to register through the tumult that continued to wrack the youth's huge form.

As suddenly as it started the seizure ended and Lorgar sat bolt upright, eyes boring holes through the metal of the wall for several heartbeats. He then turned his head and looked straight at Kor Phaeron.

'I have heard and I have seen, father!' the youth declared.

'The Powers?' Kor Phaeron let go of Lorgar's hand and backed away. 'They have communicated with you?'

'I have had a vision. I have seen and heard the Truth.' He raised a hand as though listening intently. 'And the song continues, even now.'

'What song?'

'The song of the Empyrean, of all time and space, of the universe singing to itself.'

Kor Phaeron kept all suspicion from his expression, but he did not like this turn of events. Clearly something had beset his acolyte, but he was not yet willing to believe the Powers had intervened directly.

'Rest,' he instructed the boy. He fetched the water ewer from the table and handed it to Lorgar, who drank from it as though it were a cup, downing the contents in two mouthfuls.

'It is beautiful,' said Lorgar, turning his violet eyes to Kor Phaeron. Gold flecks danced in the pupils. 'One is coming. One who will be the ending and the beginning.'

2 1 4

On being questioned further – gently, for despite his physical strength Lorgar's spirit was often still that of a frail adolescent – the acolyte revealed that he had seen a being cloaked in gold and stars, descending from the Empyrean with the wings of an eagle.

'What does it mean?' Lorgar asked. 'I can think of nothing in the Messages, nor the Observations. It cannot be the fifth prophet, can it?'

Kor Phaeron scratched his chin and moved to the door, calling for a slave to bring more water and wine, to give himself a little time to think. While he waited, he considered his options. They were few and none were to his liking.

'It is unprecedented,' he eventually admitted. Lorgar was about to speak but Kor Phaeron heard steps in the companionway and held up a hand to silence the acolyte. 'Say nothing of this yet.'

Lorgar looked as though he might protest but Kor Phaeron's glare forestalled any dissent. A knock at the door announced the arrival of a slave with a fresh jug of water and a bottle of Lanansan red. Kor Phaeron dismissed the woman and returned his attention to Lorgar, handing him the tepid water, which the youth downed in two more long draughts.

The preacher poured wine for himself and sipped, gathering his thoughts before he continued.

'If we are not sure what to make of this extraordinary event, then the Faithful will be even more perplexed. It is not our place to spread hearsay and speculation. We are ambassadors for the Truth, you are the Bearer of the Word. Until we can say unequivocally what the Powers wish us to know, what would you tell them?'

The irresistible logic cut off any retort, but Kor Phaeron did not grant Lorgar time to comment before he continued, 'We cannot ignore the timing, coincidental as it is. On this day when you speak of seeking a sign, you suffer this vision?'

'Not suffer,' Lorgar said quickly. 'It was enrapturing.'

'You looked in agony.'

'Well, yes.' Lorgar looked embarrassed, as though a guilty pleasure had been exposed. 'It was excruciating, I suppose, but so magnificent also. And now it has brought me the music of the spheres. Such a wonderful arrangement.'

'You still hear it? What does it sound like? You never heard it before? Did you hit your head when you fell?'

'Yes, wonderful, no, and no.' Lorgar's frown of chastisement made Kor Phaeron's chest tighten. 'You think I would keep this from you?'

'I do not know what to think,' Kor Phaeron said, with considerable feeling. He finished his wine with a gulp, masking an overwhelming sense of frustration. Lorgar looked to him for guidance, so guidance would be what he gave. 'But we already know that you have been marked out for greatness. I think – and this is only my initial deductions – that the vision is of yourself. It is a waking dream, a portent of what is to come. A self-revelation.'

'Like Tezen had on the slopes of Mount Ashask?'

Kor Phaeron struggled to remember the episode, his own powers of recollection far inferior to that of his acolyte. It was wise to assume the youth was right; there was not a line he could not quote verbatim.

'Of sorts,' Kor Phaeron hedged. His mind continued to race and he spoke as the words came to him, once more channelling the raw wisdom of the Powers as though from another place. 'Today you lament the absence of the Powers, and today they have sent you a vision. It is encouragement not instruction, I conclude. An inducement, perhaps, to show you what might become if you apply yourself.'

'Apply myself to what?'

Kor Phaeron hesitated. Long had he plotted this moment, for a long time unsure how he would ever achieve his goal whilst absolutely faithful to the notion that he would. Lorgar had been delivered to him for that purpose, though Kor Phaeron had only ever hinted at what he wished for his adopted son. Was it time yet?

'The Covenant, Lorgar. You are the lightbringer, the one who will push back the darkness, the purger of the faithless. The Bearer of the Word must become the principle of the Covenant, Archpriest of the Godsworn.'

* * *

2 1 5

Kor Phaeron waited with hammering heart, but he need not have feared. Lorgar considered his words only for a few moments and then nodded, radiating strength and commitment.

'Then it shall be so. We shall make for Vharadesh.'

'Now?' Kor Phaeron said, unable to hide his enthusiasm.

He was ready for the long-anticipated confrontation with his old order, had dreamed of such moments every day since his exile. The preacher knew he would only have one chance to supplant those who had so wronged him, and the new Bearer of the Word was the key to that justice. Kor Phaeron no longer professed to be master of Lorgar; he could not simply command the youth to go to the Sacred Towers, the City of Grey Flowers. Kor Phaeron met Lorgar's gaze and fell into the grip of those violet eyes.

'Not yet,' said Lorgar, 'but soon. Many answer our call, and many more will answer it in the days to come.'

'You would take an army to Vharadesh?' said Kor Phaeron, imagining the towers of his enemies being toppled, the walls of the city struck asunder by the host of Lorgar.

'I shall bring a new creed, the Truth of the One.'

'And who shall listen to the Word? A few dozen nomads, a caravan now and then? It will take more than this rabble to break the defences of Vharadesh.'

'There are those already willing to listen.' Lorgar fixed Kor Phaeron with his penetrating gaze. 'The slaves. A host of souls awaiting redemption. Two days from here lie the mines at Taranthis. We shall begin there.'

'It is blasphemy, to free slaves from bondage laid upon them by the Powers. It is not the place of…' His protest dwindled beneath the unflinching gaze of Lorgar.

'I am the Bearer of the Word, the Messenger of the Truth. Let it not be five thousand fists beating against the gates of Vharadesh, but five hundred thousand voices raised in prayer that open them.'

Against such statement, all argument fled Kor Phaeron, for Lorgar had spoken and in his voice was the Will of the Powers.

2 2 1

Little could be seen of Taranthis from the ground, for like the tezenite mine workings for which it was famed, the settlement was mostly dug beneath the hard sandstone and granite rock of the hinterlands known as the Copper Plate. Only the dark red walls of the township were visible – though the stream of heavy wagons that moved along the road between the mine and Vharadesh some one hundred and forty kilometres away betrayed its presence long before the defences came into view.

A perimeter of towers stood sentry in the dustlands several kilometres from the gatehouse, and at the approach of Kor Phaeron's caravan, columns of armoured transports issued from two of these way-keeps. Powered by efficient vapour engines, one of the prized secrets that allowed the Covenant to maintain its pre-eminence, the millipede-like transports crawled over the sands on dozens of small tracks, speargun cupolas bristling from their reticulated hulls.

Nairo watched them with a growing unease, their black flags marked with the burning book of the Covenant an unwelcome reminder of the power that had placed him into slavery.

'Axata, stand your warriors ready,' Kor Phaeron commanded from his lectern pilaster. 'Have the caravan form up.'

Armed converts lined the rails and manned the spear-hurlers of the temple-rig while flags and whistles signalled to the other vehicles to close on the mobile shrine. Nairo dodged the trampling feet and careless elbows of the soldiery, their numbers boosted further by two chance encounters in the desert while the caravan had made its way to Taranthis.

Nomad riders and chariots left plumes of sand in their wake as they rode alongside the shrine, calling to each other in their strange voices and shrill whistles. Land yachts and solar carts formed an outer ring, the whole caravan moving at the pace of the temple-rig as it ploughed through the dunes towards the incoming soldiers of the Covenant.

When the opposing groups were half a kilometre apart two trucks broke away from the Covenant contingent, flying long green pennants of parley above the flags of their church. Kor Phaeron gestured to Axata to command the temple-rig to stop, though around them the patrols continued to circle like protective silver eagles. At the masthead a green pennant was raised in reply.

The Covenant vehicles disgorged a platoon of warriors a hundred metres from the temple-rig. They were dressed in robes, the plain grey of acolytes, beneath bronzed armour plates. They carried tridents and spears, the bulky shape of slug-throwers fitted onto the hafts of the weapons beneath heads that gleamed in the Post-noon sun. Each wore a portable sun-hood that spread between two extensible poles from their backs, so that their helmed features were hidden in shade.

Another disembarked, her armour a finery of gold and rubies, a bared tulwar that gleamed with power in one fist, an archaic pistol in the other. Tendrils of semi-organic exoskeleton ran along her limbs from a backpack that clung crab-like to her form.

Nairo had never seen so much archeotech in one place. Next to him, Aladas gave him a pointed look, her eyes filled with doubt. Disconcerted mutters rippled across the deck until a growl from Axata silenced the murmuring converts.

The Covenant commander's voice rang out from amplifiers set into her helm, as loud as the hailers of Kor Phaeron.

'I am Gun-Deacon Hal Aspoa, commandant of the Third Tower. You are forbidden from approaching closer to Taranthis. If you continue on this course you will be attacked. Survivors will be subject to enslavement for their trespasses against the Holy Church of the Powers.'

Hearing a chuckle, Nairo turned to see L'sai suppressing her laugh. He glared at her.

'As if that would matter to us,' she said between stifled giggles. 'Hopefully they'll string up Kor Phaeron.'

'We'll burn with the converts, all the same,' Nairo reminded her, ending her humour.

2 2 2

Kor Phaeron watched the approach of the gun-deacon warily, arms resting on the side of the pulpit. The millicrawlers followed behind, spearguns tracking the roving outriders of his caravan. The delegation stopped about thirty metres away, a black blot on the red sands cast by their personal sunshades.

He activated the sermoniser.

'I am Kor Phaeron, seeker of the Truth, Herald of the Powers. You have no right to claim these free lands for the Covenant. You have no moral authority to deflect me from my Powers-appointed vocation.'

'The Holy Church of the Covenant extends to where its servants are, and as we are all ordained priests of the Covenant that means these are holy lands. Your blasphemy will not gain you passage. Continue and I will vouch you a heretic for the trespass.'

'Vouch away, false believer!'

The stand-off continued for several heartbeats, the two combatant priests staring at each other across the divide. A movement below drew Kor Phaeron's attention to the deck. Lorgar emerged from the shadow of the hatchway and turned to address him.

'Let me speak to them,' Lorgar said. 'Let them hear the Bearer of the Word.'

'No,' Kor Phaeron replied. 'These ingrates do not deserve to learn the Truth. Thugs in robes, nothing more. There is no more despicable thing than a traitor to the Powers masquerading as their guardians.'

'I can persuade–'

'No! You must learn an important lesson here, Lorgar. To proselytise is to invade. The act of conversion is one of spiritual violence that we must embrace. None come to the Truth on an easy road. None willingly heed the Word at first. For the soul to be pure, the flesh must endure.' Kor Phaeron switched on the address system again. 'It is you who blasphemes, haridan of Vharadesh. Depart these lands or suffer the wrath of the Powers at my hand.'

Lorgar looked to protest again but before he could speak, Gun-Deacon Hal Aspoa declared her judgement.

'You are charged with heresy, the most dire of trespasses,' she declared as more of her troops issued from their serpentine transports, electrospears snarling. Her bodyguard levelled their weapons at the temple-rig while she brought up her pistol directly towards Kor Phaeron. 'I shall cleanse your body and the Powers shall determine the fate of your soul.'

Kor Phaeron felt Lorgar move rather than saw him. He caught

the sparkle of the gun-deacon's pistol but an instant later his giant acolyte was in the way, the gleam of phased particles striking an upraised grating in his fist. In the other he had the mace he had fashioned for the pursuit of the mutineers.

Gunfire from the other guards crackled along their line and bullets whirred over the rail, met by the crack of carbines and the snap of bowstrings.

Lorgar tossed the grating discus-like into the gun-deacon's squad, felling two of them, and then vaulted over the rail.

2 2 3

Crackling ammunition from the transports' spear-hurlers and deafening shell bursts wracked the armoured side of the shrine wagon. Cowering behind a plated stanchion, shuddering at every rattle of shrapnel, Nairo peered through a hole in the metal left by a missing bolt. As when he had fought the mutineers, Lorgar became a thing of movement and energy, a stunning reminder to Nairo that the Bearer of the Word was not a mortal man but an agent of the Powers. The gun-acolytes were caught unprepared, not expecting their enemies to abandon the relative safety of the temple-rig; it would certainly have been folly for a normal human to have done so as bullets and blasts seared across the divide.

So it was that the Covenant soldiers took a few moments to react to the giant charging into their midst. Sand churned around Lorgar as he sprinted towards the gun-deacon with powerful strides. The Covenant guard leader tracked him with her pistol but her shot went astray through the flurry of grit and dust that surrounded the charging acolyte.

Lorgar met the counter-charge of the gun-acolytes with a roar that could have been the bellow of Khaane himself at the Fall of Nashesh. A sweep of his huge mace crushed the first foe into the ground while sparking tridents glanced from his skin and scorched his robes. Another swing of the mace pulped the armoured heads of two more.

Though Nairo was no expert in war he had seen enough of Axata and his ilk to recognise that Lorgar fought without training or thought. The gun-acolytes surrounded him quickly, thrusting with their tridents, aiming for the legs of the giant to fell him. Only his shocking size, speed and strength kept them at bay, forcing them back with each wild attack. Yet blow by blow they were dragging down Lorgar like lich-dogs tearing at a sternback bull.

Sooner or later a more telling strike would land.

Axata must have recognised the same, for at the instant the dread thought entered Nairo's head the commander of the converts leapt down to the sands and bellowed for his warriors to follow. Into the teeth of the Covenant fire they ploughed, spurred on by the thought of their spiritual master falling. Over their heads seared fresh volleys of fire from the spear-hurlers and Archer Brethren at the mastheads.

The crashing salvoes from the millicrawlers ceased for a moment, the gunners taken aback by this sudden offensive, unable to target the converts who sped towards their own troops. More hatches wheezed open in their flanks to disgorge fresh squads to outflank the converts pressing into the centre of their force.

Lorgar shouldered his way through the gun-acolytes to confront their leader, who ditched her pistol in favour of a two-handed grip on her tulwar. The first slashing blow scythed into the haft of Lorgar's mace, almost severing the axle. The Bearer of the Word let the weapon drop and punched a fist into her face, mashing visor and skull with a single blow, the gun-deacon's head snapped back with spine-breaking force.

Now that the concentration of fire had relented from the temple-rig, Nairo timorously stood up to look over the bulwark. A third transport was heading towards them from a more distant tower, alerted to the fighting.

Soon Lorgar and the converts would be outnumbered.

2 2 4

Fingers gripping the edge of the pulpit tight, Kor Phaeron watched with growing concern as Axata and his converts were slowly surrounded by a ring of robed Covenant thugs. The guns of the transports had turned to targeting the solar yachts and patrol wagons, forestalling any aid from the mobile elements of the caravan. The same sprawl of melee that prevented the millicrawlers from targeting Lorgar and his companions also shielded the Covenant soldiers from the weapons crews of the temple-rig.

Lorgar did his best, fighting now with a scavenged electro-spear in each hand, but as gifted as he was with tongue and mind, as fearsome as his bulk and Powers-gifted speed, he was an unwieldy fighter, and the press of foes and friends hampered his broad, swinging attacks. Already a dozen converts lay dead or bleeding on the sands, though twice that number of gun-acolytes had paid a similar price at the hands of the converts and the Bearer of the Word. But it was not enough, and it would not be long before the transport dispatched from the third tower would arrive to swing the balance decidedly against Kor Phaeron's followers.

'Not like this,' he growled to himself, before he raised his voice to address those remaining on the temple-rig. 'Not like this, brethren and sistren! The glory of the Truth does not die today on some unmarked field of sand and dirt! The Powers favour us still, if we are to seize the moment. All is a test, and we shall rise to each challenge. Cursed is the man or woman who stands by to let our dreams fail today. In the abyss will wander the souls of those who save themselves rather than see the Truth delivered to the unbelievers.'

Incensed now, righteousness replacing unease, Kor Phaeron all but threw himself down the ladder from the pulpit. Filled with vigorous energy from the Powers, inspired by the sight of the Bearer of the Word beset by a ring of foes, the priest searched about for a weapon. At the rail lay a wounded convert, her robes reddened with escaping blood, fusil lying on the deck beside her. He snatched up the longrifle and held it over his head, glaring at the slaves around him.

'If you would be messengers of the Truth, be ready to give your lives for it!'

And with that he dashed to the ladder and started to climb down to the sands, not caring whether any chose to follow. For victory or defeat, if the Powers willed it, so it would be.

2 3 1

On reflex, Nairo took a step after Kor Phaeron. A hand grabbed his wrist and he spun around to find L'sai holding him, her eyes wide and intent.

'Let them die,' she insisted, letting go. 'Let them all kill each other.'

The former teacher hesitated and looked around the deck. Several dozen slaves watched him and L'sai, ready to take their lead from one or the other. He cast his gaze out to the continuing swirl of fighting on the sands, and to the figure of Kor Phaeron striding purposefully towards the chaos. There was no hesitation there. Was Nairo any lesser man?

'Why would you give your life for him?' asked L'sai, thinking that she guessed his thoughts. 'He is nothing to us!'

'Not him.' Nairo moved his eye to the giant form of Lorgar just as the acolyte lanced one of his spears through the chest of a Covenant enforcer, bodily lifting the gun-acolyte into the air. 'For him.'

There was a look of pain in L'sai's expression. She shook her head and addressed the others.

'This moment will come again even if we live today. The

Church of the Covenant will not let this lie. Heretics they'll call us. Not just slaves, lower even than we are now. A lingering painful death at the hands of the excruciators and penance-deacons.' Her face changed, taking on a more conniving look as a thought occurred. 'Better yet, let us aid the Covenant, the better to cement our dedication to the Church of Vharadesh!'

'No,' said Nairo. He spoke quietly but quickly, seized by urgency, the thought of moments passing that could bring doom like a fist about his heart. 'No, we do not do that, for we do not answer to the Covenant but to the Powers. Believe what you may about the lives and rules of mortals, but the Powers exist and they will judge us today. Kor Phaeron is right, we stand beneath their gaze. See Lorgar! See the Bearer of the Word, the gift of the Powers to us. Think not of today but of all the days to come, and ask if that isn't worth fighting for, and even dying for?'

L'sai moved to interpose herself between him and the ladder but Nairo shoved her aside and stooped to pick up a wrench that had been discarded upon the deck. He saw others arming themselves with improvised weapons from among the corpses and blood of their companions, or looting the bodies of dead converts.

'Who do you think you are?' L'sai laughed scornfully. 'You are just a slave to them.'

'I am no slave. I have a name, and he knows it,' he replied, staring at Lorgar. He held aloft the wrench as though he wielded the mythical golden blade of Pir Olourius itself. 'I am Nairo!'

2 3 2

It took about ten heartbeats, ten lung-burning, chest-pounding heartbeats for Nairo to realise he had no idea what he was doing. As bullets spat past and the slaves to his left and right were scythed down by blasts and spear volleys, the wrench in his hand felt impossibly heavy. His strides became laboured, the sand tugging at his legs, feet made of clay as he tried to forge across the dunes that had become the centre of the battlefield.

He fixed his eyes on Lorgar, about forty metres ahead, and put his head down, ignoring the whisper of arrows and the shouts of his companions – shouts cut horribly short.

His bare feet stumbled on sharp stones and pieces of shrapnel in the sand, causing him to falter and then fall as the shock wave from a shell detonation swept over him from the right, heat and sound that blocked out all sense.

Gritting his teeth he dragged himself up, determined that if he was to die, it would be on his feet.

This is ridiculous, part of his brain cackled at him. You're a teacher. A slave. You're going to die here unmourned.

The thought spurred him on. He knew that today his life had meaning, more than in the academy cloister, certainly more than when polishing and sanding and labouring on the temple-rig.

Lorgar was covered in cuts, his robes in rags, blood coating arms and bared chest with a wash of crimson.

Yet he stood and fought on.

The gigantic acolyte, now flanked by Axata and several other converts, slashed and battered all who came before him. Even in the short time since the battle had begun in earnest his movements had become more fluid, his fighting less wild and more cultured. He thrust the spears with short stabs, gutting and piercing with faultless accuracy.

One of the transports crashed towards the melee, its crew no longer caring whether they injured allies as well as enemies, intent only on bringing down the giant who continued to defy the will of the Covenant.

Its course brought it ploughing along the ridge of the dune, directly towards Nairo and the other slaves. Small arms from visor-like slits coughed burning bolts into the mass of disorganised fighters. Nairo saw Husan's hair set aflame, flailing into the dirt. Gor Daos lost a leg to a flurry of burning projectiles that seared bone as easily as flesh. L'sai...

He had not thought L'sai would follow, but there she was, snarling and howling like a beast, a stolen glaive in her hands as she faced down the metal serpent bearing down upon them. Nairo saw her cast a glance towards Lorgar, and then she broke into a run, heading directly for the transport.

A cannon in the nose of the millicrawler belched alchemical fire and in an instant L'sai and three others with her were nothing more than steam and hissing gobbets splashed across a pool of cooling glass.

Nairo felt her death like a stab in the gut.

The sensation continued and something wetted his thighs. He looked down and realised that it was a literal wound; a short, barbed projectile stuck out beneath his ribs. Blood flowed and his legs weakened.

Again he fell into the sand, the wrench dropped from twitching fingers. The bulk of the millicrawler laboured towards him, plumes of smoke issuing from its stacks, the dune shifting and trembling under its weight, slides of sand cascading towards the vehicle as it mounted the slope.

Nairo floundered in the red-and-grey particles, possessed by the idea that the Powers would look upon him more kindly if he died with a weapon in hand. He thought of the Prophets and of the Pilgrimage into the Empyrean to bring forth the light of the Truth. Would he go there also, or into the nothingness and torment of the abyss?

The shadow of the millicrawler's nose fell upon him. He could smell the vapour fumes from its engine and the stink of grease through the blood and charred flesh. Beyond an armoured slit he saw the driver's face, eyes looking at something else, utterly unaware of the life he was about to crush from existence.

2 3 3

A sudden storm of sand raked across Nairo's face, obscuring what happened next, though he heard well enough the titanic impact and the following scream of twisting, tearing metal. Wiping tears and grit from his face, the slave saw the nose of the crawler torn open, ripped along its length, the legs of the driver still in his seat, his upper half missing.

He turned at movement in the corner of his eye and saw a giant figure sprawled on the sand a few metres away, cocooned in an elongated crater like a crashed meteor. He held two warped strips of bloodstained metal in his hands, the skin and flesh of his arms shredded from wrist to elbow.

'Lorgar!' Nairo rose, ignoring the stab of pain in his abdomen.

The acolyte roused, sitting up with the air of one not wholly in control of his senses. He said something in a tongue that Nairo didn't understand. It sounded like he could be cursing, but the slave was not sure. Lorgar tossed away the pieces of millicrawler while Nairo scrambled down the dune, following the blood-spattered course of Lorgar's descent. Shouts caused him to glance over his shoulder, where Kor Phaeron, Axata and the converts were falling back to form a position around the wrecked transport. Doors hissed open along its length. The soldiers inside staggered out to be confronted by a wave of slaves who swept over them and poured into the broken millicrawler.

Nairo staggered to a stop a couple of metres from the Bearer of the Word. Lorgar winced as he tried to stand, crimson pumping from the lacerations across the blood vessels in his arms. He grimaced as he tried to flex fingers with frayed tendons. Nairo felt a stab of conscience at the sight of the youth in pain. For so long he had thought him impervious; had he really suffered through all of those whippings and beatings in silence whilst feeling every blow?

Lorgar held up his ruined hands towards Nairo, as if pleading for something. His mouth opened and closed with a wordless appeal.

2 3 4

Nairo tore off such garments as he had, a short toga of dirty, poorly woven linen. He used the bandages to bind Lorgar's arms, while around them the battle continued to rage.

Lorgar nodded silently, focus returning to his gaze. Already the cuts across his chest and face were scabbed over, the stream of fluid from his arms stifled by his extraordinary body.

'Why?' Nairo asked. 'Why suffer so for me?'

Lorgar replied in a lilting tongue, perhaps not realising that he spoke some other language. It was impossible to read his expression, and before Nairo could ask again the Bearer of the Word surged up the dune, taking up a snapped stanchion, its sheared end as sharp as any spear. He stopped and looked back, fixing Nairo with his penetrating gaze, pinning him to the spot with its intensity.

'I might ask the same,' Lorgar said before breaking into a run, heading for the thickest fighting.

Nairo sat down, holding a hand to the wound below his ribs. It was not so severe as he had first feared; shock had wounded him more than the projectile itself. He then realised that the barb had been pulled free. He saw it lying among the other debris where the Bearer of the Word had come to a stop.

The only explanation was that Lorgar had removed it at some point even as Nairo had been helping the youth; so fast that the slave had neither seen nor felt the extraction, despite the obvious damage to the youth's hands and the pain he must have felt.

'That's why,' Nairo whispered to himself.

2 4 1

Though there was little enough of Taranthis to be seen on the surface, the trio of armoured portals that broke the rocky promontory above the mines were imposing enough. Each was a keep, independent of the others above ground, a bastion of ruddy stone and dark metal built around a gate solid enough to withstand the simple weapons of the caravan.

The guards of the outer towers, having witnessed the victory of the Bearer of the Word over those who had moved against him, had withdrawn into their mother-town, locking down their fortifications to abandon the surface to the interlopers. The cost of the victory had been considerable, some forty slaves and half as many converts in all lost, several dozen of each injured, many unlikely to survive without expert attention and facilities. A price worth paying, in Kor Phaeron's view, to teach Lorgar the nature of the opposition he would now face if he wanted to confront the Covenant.

'What do we do now?' Axata asked as he, Lorgar and Kor Phaeron stood in the shade of the golden solar-sails of two wagons, about half a kilometre from the closest barbican. 'We cannot breach Taranthis with fusils and spear-hurlers.'

'One of the sentry posts might prove an easier lair to prise open,' said Kor Phaeron. 'We will find heavier weapons within.'

'And do we have the time?' the convert leader continued. 'The Covenant have the means to speak on the air – reinforcements from Vharadesh will be here within two days.'

To this Kor Phaeron had no answer save a glowering look.

Lorgar was deep in thought, one finger held to his lips in contemplation. Standing right next to Axata, it was obvious how large he had become – half a head taller than the chieftain, and still showing no signs of his extraordinary growth abating. The Bearer of the Word had torn away the rags the slave had bound around his arms, tatters of cloth still caught in the thick scabs of his Powers-gifted blood that sheathed his forearms. They fluttered in the wind like ribbons, flaking dried crimson like rust.

'We have all that we need already,' declared Lorgar. 'Bring forward the shrine.'

'We have nothing to break rock nor melt or crack thick metal,' argued Axata.

'Ramming the gate is pointless, if that is what you have in mind, and it would be folly to strand ourselves here in the attempt,' said Kor Phaeron.

'There is no need to breach a gate that is already open,' Lorgar said cryptically, raising a hand for the temple-rig to advance. He directed a meaningful look at Kor Phaeron as he continued. 'One voice shall suffice where the mightiest weapons falter.'

2 4 2

Additional generators and speakers were brought aboard the great wagon of Kor Phaeron, to boost the amplification of the pulpit's address system. The hiss of static set the dunes vibrating and the rest of the caravan retreated a safe distance away in anticipation of Lorgar's booming address. Kor Phaeron and a handful of slaves remained, to oversee the technicalities of running the device. Nairo was among them.

He waylaid the Bearer of the Word as he approached the pulpit, while Kor Phaeron was still below. Laying a hand on Lorgar's immense bicep, he gave a nod.

'I haven't yet had time to thank you for saving my life.'

'I can recall everything,' Lorgar replied. He leaned close and dropped his voice. 'Everything you ever did and told me. Everything that passed on this rig from the moment I set foot upon it. The talk of the guards, the whispers of the slaves. Your past as a teacher, the things you taught me… I think I understand now what Kor Phaeron meant when he punished me for learning the words but not the meanings. I can recall everything anyone has said to me since I was found in the desert, but your words I *choose* to remember.'

Nairo was not sure how to reply to this, but was struck by sudden concern.

'I think Kor Phaeron would rather fight and fail, than seek victory in peace.' The slave looked over the rail to the citadel in the distance. 'And he may be right. I don't think even you could convince the guards to open the gates when they think on what we have just done to their companions.'

'You will see, Nairo, how well I remember, how well I have learned.' He patted the slave on the shoulder, the gesture gentle despite the huge hand that performed it. 'My words are not for the guards.'

Nairo watched Lorgar pull his bulk into the confines of the pulpit. Kor Phaeron emerged from below, sending Nairo scuttling away with a snarl and scowl. Circling the deck, the preacher made his way to the rail behind the driver's cab and ascended in the shade of the compartment, to watch the gatehouse in the distance. The rest of those still aboard the temple-rig bound pads of rags over their ears.

With a crack like thunder and the hiss of a thousand serpents, Lorgar activated the address system.

2 4 3

'Slaves of Taranthis, heed my words. I am Lorgar, the Bearer of the Word, messenger of the Powers, herald of the Truth. I come to you today with glad tidings, for the gaze of the Powers has fallen upon you. One is coming, one who shall set us all free from the bondage of ignorance.

'It is not the yokes and manacles that bind you to this place, it is the fear that has been set in your hearts by the doctrines of the Covenant. The mysteries of the Empyrean have been hidden from you, cloaked in ritual and obscure language. The Ecclesiarch and his priesthood have placed themselves between you and the Powers, denying you that which is in your own extent to achieve.

'I come not as one who will bring you to the Truth, for it is already in you. I, Lorgar, am not your saviour, for you do not need saving but from your own inhibitions. Each man and woman who hears these words knows of their righteousness and their own place in the gaze of the Powers. Be thankful then that into your hands have been placed the means for deliverance.

'Show now your faith, your dedication to His cause, and the One shall descend from the Empyrean to spread the light of the Truth upon us all. He does not see slaves and masters, for there is only the One above to serve, and all beneath are the servants. Not in your station shall you be judged but in your deeds. Not for the weaknesses of the past shall you be abandoned, but accepted for the strength of the present and the promise of the future.

'Vengeful we shall be against those who trespass against the One, but in love and benevolence shall He arrive, and garbed in the blazing glory of the Powers the One shall walk among us, bringing peace and purpose to our hollow existence.

'I do not call on you to do anything save that which the One has already placed in your hearts. The One demands nothing but your prayers and love. We shall rid ourselves of these odious sacrifices and free ourselves from the ignominy of false servitude. The church shall be reborn and the greatness of Colchis shall be restored, in the eyes of mortals and Powers alike.

'Strike, strike now, for eternity beckons. Be pure of faith and strong of heart, and trust your soul to the love of the One.

'We have nothing to lose but our chains!'

2 4 4

For the remainder of Mornday and into Long Noon, until the rest-eve at the height of the sun's strength, Lorgar spoke, pausing for no rest, nor food, only to take an occasional mouthful from the water bottle he had with him. The others of the caravan dozed and attended to such duties as were absolutely necessary – the converts took shifts to keep watch for any movement of the Covenant soldiers, patrolling close to the highway that was now deserted so that they might see the first sign of a response from Vharadesh.

Wake-rise of Post-noon came, the sun bright and sharp in a cloudless sky, ready to burn through the will of the hardiest soul.

Lorgar stopped talking, rousing Nairo from a half-doze that had taken him as he sat with his back against the base of the pulpit tower, ears still bound against the deafening volume of the prayer hailers.

The Bearer of the Word held a hand above his eyes, peering against the glow of the rising sun. Nairo followed his gaze, likewise shielding himself from the brightness of the lowering orb, as though staring back into the gaze of the Powers themselves. There was something different about the nearest gatehouse, though the wall facing the caravan was still shrouded in shadow.

With an involuntary shout, Nairo realised that the silhouette had changed and there was movement in the shadow.

His call woke others, including Kor Phaeron, who dashed to the ladder that led to the roof of the driver's cabin, hauling himself on top with much flapping of robes. He pointed a spindly finger towards the gate of Taranthis.

'Praise the Powers!' the priest declared. 'See how the Truth knows no barriers!'

And it was so.

Across the sands poured a tide of ragged creatures, laughing and shouting with joy. Dressed in tatters, the men and women were skeletal-limbed and pot-bellied from malnourishment, but the energy of their escape was remarkable. Dozens, then hundreds, then thousands burst forth from the mines. Many fell into the sands and lifted their hands up in supplication to the sun they had not seen for long years. Others wandered dazed over the wastes, unable to comprehend the nature of freedom.

2 4 5

Kor Phaeron quickly identified a knot of the Taranthian slaves heading directly towards the temple-rig, fifty or sixty in number. He could see that they wore looted armour and bore weapons taken from their guards – ringleaders no doubt. Men and women likely to have their own agenda above the simple fact of freedom.

He called for Axata as he descended to the main deck of the rig, and then beckoned to Lorgar. The Bearer of the Word clambered down from the pulpit, weary in body from his oratory, his passion momentarily spent despite his superhuman stamina.

'Assemble a greeting party,' Kor Phaeron told Axata, directing the convert's attention to the incoming group. 'Take water and a little food. Say nothing of Lorgar, but bring them to me.'

Axata looked as though he would disagree, looking to Lorgar for support. Kor Phaeron bit back a remark, sure in the knowledge that this was no time to rile his second-in-command. Lorgar shook his head.

'Do as Kor Phaeron bids. Extend our welcome. Introduce them to him and keep my nature quiet. We do not yet know whether they will be allies or enemies.'

'Surely they have heard the Bearer of the Word and come to offer their service, as have we all?' said Axata.

'Perhaps,' Kor Phaeron answered quickly, before Lorgar, 'but they are desperate folk and who can say what drives a person in such circumstance. Go, bring them to us.'

When Axata had gathered the soldiers he needed and led them down to the sands, Kor Phaeron took Lorgar aside.

'Wise words,' he said. 'Our people must be united. We have seen first-hand the dangers of factions growing within our camp.'

'Indeed, and I will always stand by your shoulder,' replied Lorgar.

'We must do better than that, or what we have started today will become a tide that will wash us away. We are a movement now, growing in number, and others shall be jealous of that. They will try to divide us, you and I. They will take what we have built and pervert it to their mortal ends, and the Covenant will claim it for themselves – the foundations of a new tyranny in the name of a flawed Ecclesiarch.'

He could see his words sinking into the mind of Lorgar, and pushed home his message.

'We have one opportunity, just one chance to topple the corrupt church and we cannot let others take it from us. More blood will be spilt, but the Powers shall not allow such sacrifices to be in vain. Eternity is the reward for those who die in the name of the Truth.'

'So what do you propose we do?'

'We are as one. As the Ecclesiarch is the spiritual head of the Covenant, so he has the Archdeacon of Vharadesh to attend to the practical matters. You are the Bearer of the Word, the Ecclesiarch-to-be. I shall be your archdeacon. Axata is our gun-deacon prime. As such shall all newcomers know us. To me their bodies. To you, their souls. Inseparable. Indefatigable. Victorious.'

Lorgar smiled.

'In the name of the Truth and the One.'

Kor Phaeron fought back his instinctive deflection, even though he feared his adoptive son verged on blasphemy. The visions had continued, intensified, and Lorgar was convinced that a new Power was rising to sweep away the Covenant. Perhaps there was something to be learned still.

'For the Truth, and the One,' Kor Phaeron assured him.

2 5 1

Nairo knocked on the door of Kor Phaeron's chamber and waited, casting a glance over his shoulder at his companion. Hu Osys was the appointed spokeswoman of the Taranthians, one of those who had roused the slaves at the dimly heard words of Lorgar, filled with a zealous fire by the oratory of the Bearer of the Word. Even now she had an agitated, wild manner about her as she gazed in awe at her surrounds.

'This is the sanctum,' Hu Osys whispered. 'Where Lorgar and Kor Phaeron commune.'

Nairo nodded, not sure whether to laugh at this or be afraid of the newcomers' fervour. A day and a half had passed since they had freed themselves from the mine. A wearying time in which they had trekked into the deserts to elude any potential pursuit from the forces of the Covenant. Dust caked the half-naked body of Hu Osys, her broken fingernails filled with dirt, hair matted with sweat and sand. Bathing was unthinkable; such water as they had was needed to drink.

Opening the door, Kor Phaeron was a picture of similar dishevelment. His cheeks and chin were stubbled, as was his head, and streaks of grime marked his hands and arms where he had washed in dirty water. He looked at Nairo as if noticing a bug crawling upon the deck and then turned his dismissive gaze to Hu Osys.

'Who is it?' Lorgar asked from within the chamber. 'Let them in.'

'Nairo and one of our new brethren,' Kor Phaeron said, stepping back, his irritation at playing the part of doorman to former slaves marked clearly in his expression. Lorgar was sat in a large chair, fashioned for his bulk, beside the cot that was serving as a desk for a variety of tomes and papers arranged carefully on the folded sheet. Nairo saw several parchments covered in the neat cuneiform he knew to be Lorgar's script. Looking to the shelf he saw more, several dozen in fact. At Kor Phaeron's insistence, Nairo and others had embroidered the glyphs of priesthood on the grey acolyte robes of Lorgar, to symbolise his rise to that rank, though no ordaining of the Covenant had occurred. In scarlet and cerulean, along hem and cuff and upon the chest, the symbols of the orthodoxy of Vharadesh had been replaced with symbols devised by Lorgar himself – declarations of the Truth, as the Prophet of the One, and the Bearer of the Word.

Nairo bowed his head in supplication while Hu Osys fell to her knees, forehead pressed to the flaking grey paint on the metal floor.

'Forgive this intrusion into your studies, Bearer of the Word,' began Hu Osys. Lorgar looked at Nairo with a questioning frown. Nairo shrugged in reply. The ways of the Taranthians were not his responsibility. 'We have a boon to ask of you, speaker of the Truth.'

'Ask it,' said Lorgar, setting aside his autostylus to put his hands in his lap. 'And please get up.'

* * *

2 5 2

Hesitantly, Hu Osys regained her feet, hands clasped to the simple rope belt that held her skirt at the waist. The cudgel of a Covenant mineguard hung at her hip, carried more as a trophy than a weapon.

'There are five thousand of us that fled Taranthis, learned ones,' she said. 'Though we brought such water and rations as we were able in the time we had to depart, our supplies are perilously low. I wondered if you might tell us how long we must endure until we reach where we are going?'

Lorgar looked at Kor Phaeron to answer.

'Another two days, if you can keep up,' said the archdeacon of the Truth. 'We head for Meassin, where Covenant thugs oversee plantations of cotton and flax. Ten thousand labour beneath their whips in the fields and mills to spin yarn and weave linen for the impious hypocrites of Vharadesh. A ripe harvest for the Bearer of the Word.'

At this Hu Osys looked dismayed and held her hands to her face.

'We have not the food nor water for such a journey, great leaders,' she said, looking imploringly from Kor Phaeron to Lorgar. 'The desert is no place to feed five thousand mouths.'

'What would you have us do?' snapped Kor Phaeron. He waved a hand towards the loaves and ewers set on a table beside Lorgar. 'Conjure food and wine from the meagre supplies we have for ourselves?'

'I can do without, for a while,' said Lorgar. He reached towards the platter.

'Even your appetite does not match that of five thousand,' countered Kor Phaeron. 'The Powers do not give their boons freely, as much as we call them gifts. Their gratitude is earned, through ordeal and proving one's faith.'

Lorgar nodded sadly, withdrawing his hand while his gaze settled upon Hu Osys.

'My archdeacon is right. This is no path to be trodden by the weak-willed. Two days. At Meassin we will pause and you shall drink at the wells and feed at the trenchers of the Covenant. Share what you have, as you deem fitting. Pray and know that your actions take you closer to the Truth. Those the Powers judge worthy will survive.'

He returned to his books, silently dismissing his audience. Hu Osys nodded numbly and withdrew with shuffling steps, muttering thanks to the Bearer of the Word for his wise counsel.

2 5 3

Nairo stood at the threshold, aware of the contemptuous look that Kor Phaeron directed at him.

'You have something else to say?' asked the archdeacon.

If he was ever to speak up, to test the new-founded supposed egalitarian ideology of the One, now was as good a time as any.

'Lorgar, we have supplies in the caravan that we could share with the Taranthians. The nomads can hunt…' His voice trailed away as he noticed that the Bearer of the Word was sitting immobile, his gaze distant, the only movement being the breath in his chest.

'Another Long Noon and Post-noon at most, that is all they will gain from it,' said Kor Phaeron. 'The painful decisions must still be made, the testing must still be undergone. What are you staring at?'

The archdeacon turned and his mood changed instantly, his belligerence draining away to be replaced with something like sorrow. Anger quickly returned as Kor Phaeron shoved Nairo out of the door.

'Leave!'

'What is he doing?'

Kor Phaeron's voice dropped to a harsh whisper.

'Communing with the One. Leave us! Speak not of this to anyone else, or brotherhood or not I shall see your skin hanging as a flag from the mast.'

The door slammed in Nairo's face a moment before he heard a muffled low moaning, swiftly followed by indistinct words of comfort from Kor Phaeron. Dismayed, Nairo retreated along the companionway, unsure what to think of the episode.

2 5 4

To see someone as vital, so physically imposing as Lorgar in pain was dreadful. The Bearer of the Word clasped his hands to his temples, eyes screwed shut, jaw clenched as he rocked back and forth on his chair. Kor Phaeron didn't even know what he was saying; he just let a stream of words fall from his lips, hoping Lorgar could hear them. Offering comfort and support though it looked as though the Powers drove hot nails into Lorgar's brain.

A test, he reminded himself. All accomplishment was achieved through adversity. Pain was the wage of the mortal, the price paid on the route to immortality.

With a last grunt, Lorgar straightened and opened his eyes, his gaze still glassy and distant. Now came the reward and the smile that crept across his face was sublime, the pleasure so infectious that Kor Phaeron could not help but grin to witness it. It seemed even more intense than on previous occasions.

He picked up one of the water ewers and stood ready.

Lorgar shuddered visibly and his soul returned to the senses of the mortal shell in which it normally resided. Kor Phaeron could not imagine what these travels into the Empyrean were like to experience, and Lorgar had been oddly reluctant in his discussions.

Now he looked at his archdeacon with a glint in his eye, an energy Kor Phaeron had not seen since he had decided to take on the Covenant at Taranthis.

'We are vindicated, father,' said Lorgar. In these vulnerable moments he lapsed into the patriarchal appellation, but Kor Phaeron was used to it now and let it pass unremarked. Lorgar took the water with a grateful nod and downed the contents. He grinned more widely. 'The Powers have sent me a new vision.'

'New?' Kor Phaeron asked the question lightly but the declaration set his heart fluttering. The first vision had set them on this course towards confrontation with the Covenant. Was Lorgar about to change his mind, to speak of a new destiny? 'Not a vision of the One?'

'He was there, as before. Gold and light personified. Another was with Him.'

'The One have become the Two?'

'A magus, robed in blue, like the drawings of the ancient shamans. With a single eye, gazing with the brightness of the Powers, seeing all.'

'A golden god and a wise man,' said Kor Phaeron. 'Vindication indeed! The Powers assert the Truth again, assuring us that we tread the path. You will be the golden one and I the magus.'

'I think that is so,' said Lorgar, laying a hand on Kor Phaeron's shoulder. The priest trembled at the thought and tears misted his vision.

'I had always believed…' He knelt, holding Lorgar's massive hand in his. 'I knew that I did the work of the Powers. Others scorned me, but still I knew that the Truth would be known. Through you, Lorgar, it shall be.'

'Through *us,*' said Lorgar. 'We must preach the Word of the One, and the Truth will return to Colchis.'

And I shall be archdeacon of the Covenant, thought Kor Phaeron, risen to my rightful station as lord of Vharadesh.

2 6 1

From Meassin on to Ahesh Ahuk, and thence to Kofus on the lava plains of Toursas, the followers of Lorgar travelled from encampment to encampment, quelling such armed resistance as was raised against them and speaking to the freed slaves. Ten thousand, twenty thousand, thirty thousand numbered the host of the One by the time they liberated the internees of the plantations at Seasas and Ouresh.

The number of the gathering devotees proved problematic, as it had after Taranthis, and a semi-permanent camp was set at Merina where the greater part of the Faithful remained while Lorgar took the core of the converts into the deeper desert, ever driven on by his visions to pave the way for the arrival of the One.

'It is not enough that we break the shackles of slaves. There are others who have sought succour from the Covenant and been rejected,' Lorgar told Kor Phaeron after the Bearer of the Word had announced that they would once more be heading for The Sands that Slay.

'There is nothing of worth in the Low Barrens,' Kor Phaeron replied, but Lorgar simply smiled. The archdeacon would not accept this. 'You would recruit more of the Declined? That would take an age. The slaves come to us a thousand, three thousand at a time. The nomads of the wastes live in tribes no more than three, four hundred strong. Were you even to find them, we would waste all our resources on the recruitment. This plan is folly, Lorgar. We should head next for Ghastaresh, to the salt flats.'

Lorgar would not be swayed though, and in his calm manner insisted that they would head into the Low Barrens at the following wake-rise, which would herald the next Dawnaway.

The journey was not so storm-ridden as the first, though winds raged and sands stripped paint from metal and timbers with a fury that flayed uncovered flesh. When asked where they were heading Lorgar would not reply directly, saying only that he was being guided by the One. Kor Phaeron continued to comfort him as repeated visions assailed Lorgar's waking thoughts – always of the golden warrior and the robed magus, which the archdeacon took as a sign that the Powers were still content with the course their messengers had taken.

Then they came upon the expanse known as the Crater of Sorrows: forty kilometres across, scarred into the wastes in a bygone age and littered with the debris of a broken skycity. Rich pickings for any who dared its rim, but such treasure hunters were few and far between for the crater was cursed by the Powers, haunted by a drake-beast that lived beneath the sands and devoured entire expeditions.

The nomads had many names for the monster, whose presence forced them to divert by a day and more on their journeys between the oases at Fourrh, Khornasa, Al Nerga and Ashadsa.

Khaane's Serpent it was called, and the Doom of Cities. Mostly it was known in Declined legend as the Kingwyrm.

* * *

2 6 2

It was with some anxiety that the caravan crossed the ridged rock into the bowl of the crater early one Mornday. Patrol yachts and lookouts scoured the sands for any sign of the diabolic creature. At word from Lorgar they left their vehicles on rocky ground and ventured out on foot, swathed in robes and carrying thick shades against the strengthening sun.

The winds swiftly eradicated all trace of their route, but the slowly rising orb of the Powers gave them the means to navigate for the heart of the Crater of Sorrows. Some four kilometres they had traversed when there came a shout from scouts on sunstriders riding a few hundred metres ahead.

Lorgar spied it next with his immortal eyes, but it was only moments before Kor Phaeron saw that which had raised the alarm.

A ridge of sand, near ten metres high, ploughing through the dunes on a course parallel to their own. Axata called the several hundred to order, at first gathering them en masse to meet the Kingwyrm as they watched its course change, circling around them now that they had stopped. How it knew of their position was impossible to tell.

'No!' Lorgar called out to them. 'Spread out. Give it no single target.'

Heeding these wise words, the converts split into smaller groups, putting several dozen metres between themselves as the bulge in the ground that was the Kingwyrm turned sharply and arrowed towards them. At the centre stood Lorgar, mace in his hands, shade discarded so that he might move freely, sweat running in thick rivers from his bald scalp. His skin was the colour of liquid gold in the low sunlight, inhuman muscles bulging beneath.

About half a kilometre distant, the hump in the sands disappeared.

* * *

2 6 3

With the progress of their foe hidden from sight, the converts started to panic, shouting to each other to see if its course had been spied, moving closer together again, instinctively seeking the protection of the group.

'Keep your distance!' roared Lorgar, but his warning came too late.

In a spume of broken rock and red sands a hundred metres high the Kingwyrm erupted from the desert depths, its fanged maw open to swallow two dozen converts amidst several tonnes of grit and ash. With a crash that sent ripples flowing through the sands, the monstrous beast fell upon the surface, crushing another thirty men and women beneath its bulk.

Kor Phaeron stood rooted to the spot, never in his life having faced anything so terrifying. Here was the wrath of the Powers incarnate and his first thought was for the wrongs he had done them with his lip service to Lorgar's sermons of the One. He offered up silent prayer and apology there and then, promising never to stray from the path of the Empyreal Truth again.

The Kingwyrm was neither worm nor serpent nor drake, not any creature depicted in the histories and bestiaries that Lorgar had translated for Kor Phaeron. It was near two hundred metres long, flanks shimmering with triangular scales of gold and red, each the equal in size of a warrior's full shield. Black barbs like vestigial limbs, each five metres long, studded its length, dragging it through the sands. Behind its head was a bony, frilled crest that encompassed its neck, splayed slightly and quivering, marked with rings of ochre and blue among the gold.

Three clusters of multifaceted eyes stared at the archdeacon from beneath horny brows, the sun, sand and dead warriors reflected in gem-like organs each the size of his head. The mouth split almost the length of the five-metre-long head, lined with several rows of scimitar-like teeth, black as the ambulatory barbs, dripping with thick saliva whose noxious stench could be smelt even at this distance. Broken bones and pieces of flesh from the converts wedged between the fangs alongside older pieces of rotting carcasses and the bones of animals that had wandered into the Kingwyrm's lair.

264

Axata and his warriors responded with shouts and curses while fusil blasts and explosive arrows bounced harmlessly from the Kingwyrm's thick scales. The monster thrashed its tail, flattening another score of Kor Phaeron's soldiers, carving a metres-deep furrow in the red sand.

Lorgar broke into a run, heading directly for the Kingwyrm, mace held in one hand as he accelerated to a full sprint, seeming to fly over the shifting grit dunes leaving barely a footprint in his wake.

The Kingwyrm saw him and coiled, raising its head thirty metres above the desert, silhouetted against the merciless glare of the rising sun. It swayed left and right, eyes glittering, judging the approach of its prey.

Without a sound, the Kingwyrm lunged, massive jaw falling upon the Bearer of the Word, scooping him up in a flurry of sands and shattered rock.

Kor Phaeron let out a cry of dismay and fell to his knees, his weapon falling from numb fingers. He watched in disbelief as the Kingwyrm reared up again, trailing an avalanche of sand from its jaw, straightening its neck to swallow. Similar shouts of horror and fear echoed from the converts.

Suddenly the Kingwyrm tilted its head, flexing its neck again, as though its meal had become stuck. It spasmed and threw its head sideways, crashing into the ground to smash a handful more of the converts into bloody paste. Head lolling, the monster thrashed through the dunes, its claw-barbs churning the air and sand with uncoordinated scrambling.

A ripple passed along the beast from head to tail, hurling tons of dirt into the air, a shiver that rattled the barbs while the crest fluttered for several heartbeats and then fell limp.

Kor Phaeron stared on dumbstruck as the Kingwyrm's mouth opened slowly, the jaw prised apart from within by Lorgar, who staggered out along a lolling tongue as though it were a boarding ramp, before falling face first into the sand.

Almost as one the converts and Kor Phaeron were on their feet and dashing to the aid of the Bearer of the Word.

'Don't touch me!' Lorgar warned, struggling to his feet, coated head to foot in the saliva of the Kingwyrm. His skin was sloughing away from the muscle in places, dribbles of melting fat falling to the dirt. 'Its spit burns the flesh.'

The Bearer of the Word flung himself into the sands and scraped what he could of the thick gunk from his naked body, exposed flesh raw in places when he was finished. Only then would he let Kor Phaeron tend to his wounds, with the command to Axata and the others to return to the caravan and salvage such scales and bones as they could from the huge corpse.

'And what would you do with them?' asked Axata.

'Fashion a sign,' said Lorgar, 'so that all who pass shall see that the slayer of the Kingwyrm will be found at Merina. The Word shall travel faster and farther than ever we could bear it ourselves.'

2 7 1

'What do you mean, "that's it"?' said Lorgar. He turned his massive bald head and looked down at Nairo, face screwed up with irritation. 'All I see is dust and smoke, and my eyes are far keener than yours.'

'And that is all you'll see of the fabled City of Grey Flowers this wake-main,' replied Nairo. As the two of them stood at the bow of the temple-rig, just above the forward drives, he looked at the haze of sand and clouds on the horizon. 'And on the wake-rise you will see why.'

It had been nine more days since Lorgar's defeat of the Kingwyrm, in which many Declined had flocked to the call of the one they called the *rain-caller* and *wyrmslayer.* Rimwards they had travelled, through the desert and into the Periphery, the Bearer of the Word intent upon arriving at Vharadesh as though on some unknown appointment with the Powers.

True to Nairo's word, having travelled through the rest-eve of Dawnaway, the caravan of Kor Phaeron's disciples reached the first proper roads that led to famed Vharadesh as the light of Mornday spread across the coastal clifftops.

They left the rest of the tens of thousands of Lorgar's converts behind, to make camp away from sight of the city and its defenders. Coming out of the Periphery, they met no traffic at first, for the bulk of the city's visitors came along the coastal roads from Assakhor and Tezenesh. Such traffic brought with it much grime and soot, smog and dirt, and the fume of their wake shrouded the city from wall to highest tower, so that only the vaguest outline of turrets and the high pinnacle of the main temple could be seen.

They soon reached the plains, sands miraculously turning to terraces of rice paddies and flowing cereal fields by dint of the arcane irrigation systems dug beneath the land. Set into motion by the ancestors in an untold age, the filtration and desalination systems continued to provide fresh water up to fifteen kilometres from the city, though each year brought more irreversible malfunctions and losses; in places hectares of formerly fertile land had returned to scrub and wilderness, leaving patchworks of grey and red among the yellow and green.

Slaves worked the fields beneath the gaze of pacing overseers, while the rice crops, requiring a far more attentive and loving master or mistress, were given as reward to the free farmers, in return for continued allegiance to the Covenant. Overhead, dirigibles drifted at mooring ropes, their cargoes of milled flour, dried rice and other bounty of the 'fertile arc' lifted on long ropes to be carried to Vharadesh or sent in trade to the other conurbations that clung to existence at the edge of Colchis' vast main continent.

Nairo watched the slaves, recalling the turn of the Powers' whim that had placed him under the charge of Kor Phaeron rather than beneath the whip of an oat-grower's thugs. He pointed to a nearby field of green corn, and to the men and women pulling the weeds from between the stiff rows.

'That could have been me, Lorgar,' he said. 'Kept in bondage to the Covenant, I might have lived out my days on one of these plantations.'

'But you did not, and the Powers brought you to me,' the youth replied, understanding his intent. He dutifully asked the question. 'How did you meet Kor Phaeron?'

Before Nairo could furnish the answer, a shout from the preacher drew everyone's attention. Atop the pulpit, Kor Phaeron addressed his people.

'We come nigh to the sanctuary of the serpents,' he warned them. 'Be vigilant, for the air itself is corrupted by their complacency. There is not one ally here for our message – trust none who you meet on our way. Every slave is an eye of the Covenant, every trader an ear. The name of Kor Phaeron is not welcome in these lands, and so if asked you will say that you travel under the mastery of Kor Adaon. Say nothing of our purpose, if possible, and little if not. We are simply seekers of wisdom, having completed a missionary pilgrimage in the deserts. Lorgar! Remove yourself from sight! We shall not have our arrival heralded by rumours abounding of a giant come to the Sacred Towers.'

Lorgar signalled his assent to Kor Phaeron before disappearing into the depths of the temple-rig – a feat that had become harder and harder as he had continued to gain height and mass. Even now, nearly seven feet tall, he showed no signs that he had reached his full size. He took up the berths of four slaves and ate enough for twenty. Nairo watched him go, feeling the same sudden emptiness of spirit he experienced whenever deprived of Lorgar's company.

'Make ready for our arrival, we shall be upon the gates before wake-main,' Kor Phaeron declared.

272

Vharadesh looked much as it did when Nairo had been thrown out with Kor Phaeron and his cult, an inconsequential piece of baggage like the others; the fact that they had paid no willing part of Kor Phaeron's heresy had been irrelevant.

The city was surrounded by a twenty-metre-high curtain wall of sandstone, flint and granite, much repaired in places, with the main city gate flanked by twin towers of obsidian. Beyond, through the dust and the fume of fires and engines, the spires and towers of a thousand temples rose over the line of the wall, tiled in grey and red, their bricks and stones hidden by coloured plaster.

Through the obscuring haze one could just about make out flowers, hanging in the tens of thousands from balconies and external pulpits, window ledges and roof baskets. The famed moon lily blooms for which Vharadesh was sometimes named the City of Grey Flowers and from whose petals the dyes were crushed for the robes of the priesthood.

Courier gyros buzzed back and forth, weaving between flocks of cherub gulls and temple ravens raised as messengers between the various denominations that made up the lower levels of the Covenant hierarchy.

In the distance, upon the Mount of the Prophets, the Spire Temple could be seen like a finger pointing to the Empyrean, a kilometre of white and gold, black and silver topped by a pinnacle of crystal glass. Beneath were a score of domes, each the roof to a nave capable of holding an audience of thousands, mounted by renditions of the book and the flame.

Vharadesh was grandeur of the highest order, an immaculate representation of physical holiness built along ordained protocols, so that the voices and prayers of the mortal world could be lifted to the Empyrean. It was home to a million and more souls, and thrice as many slaves who, dogma would attest, had no souls worth saving.

It was this last fact that stuck in Nairo's memory. Made a slave for testifying on behalf of a slave. Then, enslaved in turn and given to a preacher who would later be exiled for his own heresies. Nairo had spent more time as a teacher than a slave within the dark walls, yet the half-year between his indenture to Kor Phaeron and being turned out into the Barrens was one long catalogue of misery after another.

Despite all that, the city offered a genuine chance at freedom, whatever form it might take.

He swallowed his nervousness, though given the circumstances of their mission, the others would not think worse of him for showing a little unease. Axata was alert and ready to act in a moment. His converts were similarly scouring the other caravans, the mass of people and vehicles transiting along the coastal highways, accumulating in a mess of queues and camps around the gate. Overhead the supply dirigibles buzzed, the hum of their solar engines a backdrop to the growl of motors and chatter from the traders and pilgrims who flocked around the walls of the City of Grey Flowers.

Within a perimeter of city guards the converging masses became a pell-mell of beasts and carts and pedestrians all trying to pass through the space of a ten-metre-wide gateway. There was nobody to direct the traffic, and so there was much shouting and cursing, invoking of the Powers and the prophets, and general harassment.

Kor Phaeron need not have concerned himself about secrecy. The temple-rig and its escorting wagons had approached no closer than two kilometres to the wall when the crowds of trade missions, penitents and pilgrims around the gate were parted. A body of people several hundred strong emerged from the city, cutting through the wash of humanity like a knife blade aimed for Kor Phaeron.

The Covenant's rod-bearers, as they were known, were dressed in acolyte robes, but over the folds of cloth they wore carapaces of armour and visored helms. The symbolic rods they carried, black wooden staves a metre long bound with silver wire, were fitted with shock-spikes in case the crowds became too unruly, but it was the heavily armoured gun wagons at their back, the muzzles of their cannons projecting menacingly from squat turrets, that gave them true authority.

Axata and his converts deployed around the wagon, advancing ahead with their weapons showing but not drawn.

2 7 3

Nairo and the others waited for the order of Kor Phaeron, fearful but also determined. Lorgar, though not present, had made his implacable will known. First the Truth and the Word, and only after all peaceful attempts would come the swing of the mace. If the Covenant would bar their passage into the city, the servants of the One would call to the remaining thousands of the Faithful to force the issue.

'One in the Empyrean, above all others,' the former slave muttered, 'if the word of a lowly teacher is worthy of anything, please see me through this day. I have cared for your son, Lorgar, and taken his Word as my own, adopting the Truth as he has spoken it. As great as the rewards of everlasting life in the Empyrean are sure to be, I really would rather not have my mortal life ended here.'

The dark-clad rod-bearers formed up ahead of Axata and his converts, pushing aside any hope that their advance had been coincidence. The smell of exhaust fumes drifted over the wagon and made Nairo cough, then silence descended, nothing but the thud of his heart in his chest to disturb the peace.

Kor Phaeron took several steps towards the warriors of the Covenant, but before he could speak they broke ranks, forming a gap in their lines for the occupants of a shaded solar ketch.

From this transport issued forth a dozen men and women robed in the colours of priests, icons carried on backpoles that showed them to be of moderate rank within the complex and precise hierarchy of Vharadesh's church.

From another transporter came more rod-bearers, but with them they brought several biers, their contents looking like heaped blankets and sheets. They fell in behind the priests, as the entourage approached hesitantly, their eyes roving over everyone present, looking more afraid than Nairo felt.

'Where is the giant?' one asked, a shaven-headed priestess with her cheeks tattooed in dark blue, rings of office on her slender fingers.

'The Bearer of the Word is not here,' replied Kor Phaeron, responding quickly to the strange situation. 'I am Kor Phaeron, archdeacon of the One Truth.'

'I am Coadjutor Silena,' said the priestess. 'You are well known in this city, Kor Phaeron. Yet it is not to you that we have come forth. Why is the Bearer of the Word not with you?'

'I am his archdeacon,' insisted Kor Phaeron. Though he spoke with surety, Nairo could well imagine the confusion playing out in his former master's thoughts. Not only was their presence known, it was expected – yet this seemed to be a welcome, not a repulse.

'What is your purpose in detaining us in this fashion?' Kor Phaeron continued.

'You are not detained,' said Silena, shocked at the implication. She gestured for the guards with the stretchers to come forwards and the priests parted to let them. Nairo could see that each carried in fact a body, covered with a death shroud of the Covenant. A threat, perhaps? Had Kor Phaeron sent agents into the city ahead of their arrival? 'We have a gift for Lorgar.'

Axata and the others put their hands on their weapons, eyeing the rod-bearers suspiciously. Nairo tried to shrink back without moving, subtly placing a little more of the bulk of the shrine wagon between him and the Covenant's enforcers.

At a nod from the coadjutor, the guards pulled back the shrouds, revealing three men and four women, faces bloated and discoloured from strangulation, or perhaps poison. It was not their faces that drew the gasp from Nairo though, but their robes, for six wore the grey-and-white garb of hierarchs, and the seventh the dove-grey attire of the Ecclesiarch himself.

'Praise the One!' declared Silena, the call echoed by the other priests and rod-bearers. She smiled at Kor Phaeron as their shout disappeared on the growing wind. 'Your exploits precede you, archdeacon. The spirit of the One has moved amongst us. Vharadesh stands ready to receive its true lord, Lorgar the Bearer of the Word. All hail the Golden One!'

THE BROTHERHOOD

963.M30

Forty-Seven Six (formerly Therevad)

It was a pleasure to burn. There was a particular smell to burning books that put Kor Phaeron in mind of a certain winter incense that was used in the Spire Temple of the Covenant. Upon each prayer hour wisps of the fumes had risen to his office, a sign that all was progressing in a timely fashion as he had ordained.

Rich smoke filled the Vaults of Caralos. The nature of the volumes being torched made it all the sweeter for the First Captain. Volumes of Imperial lore. Books dedicated to the veneration of the Emperor. Tracts on the Imperial Truth, treatises by Remembrancers, slender pamphlets of prayers dedicated to He Who Rules Terra.

With hand flamers continuing their blazing work, the Ashen Circle moved methodically through the archives, hacking down the shelves with their axe rakes to make pyres of paper and vellum. Word Bearers Chaplains – once creators and curators of this collected wisdom – emptied flasks of clear oil no longer considered blessed, before the gathered squads turned their weapons upon the sodden mounds of shredded pages. Flames rose to the ceiling, yet the fumes and fire were no hindrance to the power-armoured warriors.

It was Lorgar's will that all trace of the Cult of the Immortal Emperor be expunged from the Legion, that the Word Bearers would remove the traces of their inglorious past from the worlds of compliance lest the Emperor make another show of doing so for them, as He had on Monarchia. If the creed of Lorgar was to be wiped from the galaxy, it would be by the hands of his own sons and no other. To do their primarch's bidding on such an important matter had brought out the most zealous of the Ashen Circle, even those who were firmly sworn to the ideals espoused by their outlawed faith in the Emperor.

Kor Phaeron gloried in the destruction for reasons not shared with most of those present. It was the end of a falsehood. It mattered not whether the Emperor was a god. He was not one of the Powers, and it was to those immortal beings he owed his first and only allegiance. The 'Old Faith', he had started calling his beliefs amongst a growing coterie of conspirators. The Brotherhood lived again, spawned from the Dark Heart of the XVII, as it had been on Colchis.

There were many who desired faith, needed it to sustain them in these troubling times. If faith in the Emperor was banned they would look elsewhere to fill the void, and it was then that Kor Phaeron had their ear.

When all in the lower vaults was aflame, Kor Phaeron signalled for his company to ascend from the depths to the surface level of the sealed vault, leaving burning ruin in their wake. They came to the main nave of the library, the accumulated scripture of a century lined upon ebon shelves. Banners depicting Lorgar crowned in the halo of the Emperor's light hung from the beams above. Eagles of gold with eyes of ruby festooned the capitals of the pillars holding up the mosaic-clad ceiling. Long scrolls inked red with litanies of devotion made streamers across shelf after shelf of books.

'A just fate, long-delayed,' stated Lieutenant-Commander Menelek. 'I never really understood why you Colchisians were so adamant that you write down everything.'

The former Imperial Herald, veteran of the Legion's origin on Terra, waved for his squads to continue the destruction. All of them bore the markings of the First Founding, their loyalty to the Emperor unquestioned for over one hundred years.

'Why did you tolerate it?' asked Jarulek, motioning for his own men to muster on him as he came up beside the lieutenant-commander. 'Our barbaric Colchisian superstitions?'

'The Emperor had not forbade it,' Menelek said in explanation. 'It is only by His censure that we act.'

'And the Will of Lorgar,' said Kor Phaeron.

Flames licked up the high stacks, catching on the banners. The snarl of chainblades reverberated across the library, punctuated by the crash of upended cabinets and splintered wood.

'The primarch is right to address his error, but the chastisement came too late. We are already diminished in the eyes of the other Legions for our tardy conquests. The necessity for this punishment will lower our standing even further. Perhaps we should even return to being the Imperial Heralds. Scour away the last of these Colchisian delusions and make the Seventeenth great again.'

'I think that settles things.' Jarulek's voice on the vox was distorted by the static of a ciphered channel.

Kor Phaeron blink-activated an icon in his display to reply on the same frequency.

'Lorgar wills it.'

The bark of Bel Ashared's bolter was harsh and sudden. The explosion of its round against the side of Menelek's helm even sharper. An instant later the library was filled with a cacophony of bolter fire, the hiss of meltaguns; through the flames sparked lascannon beams and the flare of missiles. Caught in a prepared crossfire, the former Iconoclasts were cut down, their return fire of no threat, swiftly ended.

In thirty seconds, one hundred Space Marines were felled, armour slashed, broken and shattered by the treacherous attack.

'Some of them still live,' reported Jarulek as he looked down on the form of Menelek at his feet. The lieutenant-commander weakly grabbed at the captain's greaves before being kicked away. Jarulek aimed his bolter at Menelek's head.

'No,' ordered Kor Phaeron. He gestured towards the main doors while smoke and fire continued to fill the space around them, an almost living thing. Oil flasks and flamer ammunition casks started to smoke and explode among the fallen. The moans of the wounded became curses across the vox until Kor Phaeron silenced the company link to address Jarulek and his brothers. 'Leave them among the ashes of the Emperor they failed.'

BOOK 3: INVOCATION

108 years ago [terran standard]
22.5 years ago [colchisian calendar]

3 1 1

'High Adjutor Silena, please come in.'

Kor Phaeron waved his associate to one of the plain wooden chairs that were arranged around the library. The priestess nodded her thanks and sat down. She still wore a travel cloak over her robes, dusty from her journey, her eyes ringed pale from the glare goggles now placed on her brow above her heavily tanned face. Unbidden, Axata stepped forwards carrying a tray with cups of water. The chief disciple of Kor Phaeron, now officially ranked as gundeacon-prime, wore a smooth suit of sculpted armour that whined slightly as he moved, a grey tabard denoting his rank over the black plates.

Silena took one of the plain clay goblets and swiftly downed the contents.

'Your business in Lo Shassa was successful?' the archdeacon asked. Though Axata swept the library for spyholes and archeotech devices every day, Kor Phaeron knew better than to speak openly of his plans and schemes within the walls of the Spire Temple. Though if Silena bore the news he hoped such precautions might become redundant in the future.

'I bear grave news, archdeacon,' Silena said solemnly though her expression did not match her sombre tone. 'Hierarch-vizier Jusua and his missionary caravan were ambushed in the Valley of the Red Queen. Bandits, probably, or perhaps militants from one of the other cities.'

'A shame,' said Kor Phaeron. 'Jusua and his brethren were the last of the Relic Wardens. Now I will have to appoint new chief guardians of the armouries and museums. I told him it was folly to seek to parley with the outlanders but he would not listen. In fact, the more I insisted that he did not speak with the ambassadors of Koray, the more he was determined to do so.'

'Here is that list you asked for, archdeacon,' said Axata, sliding a paper onto Kor Phaeron's desk bearing the names of favourable candidates to the now-empty positions of the three Relic Wardens.

'I heard a rumour in the city,' said Silena, dropping her voice. 'Several of those who spoke against you in the Consortium have left Vharadesh with their families and entourages. Pilgrimages, they say, but there is also word that they complain of "a dark heart" corrupting the works of the Covenant.'

'Enemies of the One,' growled Kor Phaeron. 'Let them flee to the other cities. Their pleas will fall on deaf ears after the centuries of subjugation and disrespect the Covenant has laid upon its neighbours.'

'They might yet foment rebellion against Lorgar, send agents into the church to undermine his leadership,' said Axata.

'And that is why I have entrusted the guard of this temple to you, my vigilant gun-deacon. Or perhaps I should have considered someone else?'

'No, I will see that the Bearer of the Word is safe,' the burly soldier replied. 'My life and soul are sworn upon it.'

'And I will see his works come to full fruition,' Kor Phaeron assured them. 'The Consortium convenes again in four days' time. They shall ratify Lorgar's elevation to the position of

Ecclesiarch, and the Covenant will be united in the worship of the One and the Truth.'

'Where is the Golden One?' asked Silena. 'I would receive his blessing again if possible.'

'Where he always is,' said Axata with a smile. He gestured to a heavily leaded window, beyond which spread the roofs and towers of the City of Grey Flowers. 'If not in the grand library, he is among his people spreading the True Word.'

3 1 2

The Powers work in the most arcane ways, thought Nairo.

A little over a year and a half earlier he had become a miserable slave, taken from his place as a teacher to labour in the most gruelling and degrading fashion beneath the whip of a tyrannical priest. And from thence into the desert, the property of a deluded exile.

He should have died, either by violence or from one of the many physical ailments that affect a person after long exposure to the harsh elements, yet the Powers had seen fit to carry him to this day relatively intact. From the humiliation of abject servitude to the glory of standing upon a balcony of the Spire Temple in Vharadesh, looking out across the Square of the Martyrs filled with hundreds of thousands of Faithful; at his side the Ecclesiarch of the Covenant who had personally requested – not demanded – his presence during this inauguration speech.

Lorgar looked magnificent, near three metres tall and clad in custom-made purplish-grey robes that shimmered with silken threads, a halo of gold fixed about his brow. Ostentation that he was not proud to bear but was demanded of him by custom and the expectations of the masses. On the far side stood Archdeacon Kor Phaeron, as malignant and destructive as the day Nairo had first met him, but safe within the shadow of his adoptive son.

Lorgar raised his massive hands and the hubbub of the crowd silenced immediately, leaving only the cries of the crows and gulls that circled the many spires of the grand temple. Nairo felt his heart stop for an instant, caught up in the moment. His faith had been rewarded with this opportunity to stand at the side of the Bearer of the Word, to share in his victory.

3 1 3

'Blessing of the One upon this gathering,' Lorgar declared. 'Long have I thought of this moment, since I was a child plucked naked from the desert, though I did not ever hope to see the rise of the One so furnished in the glories of the Covenant. We have achieved something great this day, something that will forever change the lives of everyone in Vharadesh and its environs.

'As free people, as a single congregation united under the One Truth, we have put aside our competing philosophies, cast aside the superstition of the old ways to set our feet upon a road to enlightenment and renewed prosperity. You have travelled this journey with me, and my heartfelt thanks cannot convey the gratitude with which I am filled, nor the humbling nature of your support.

'No more shall we sacrifice each other for the vainglory of ego and the cold promises of mortals. Divided were the oxen pulling the yoke in different directions, straining against each other in the hopes of digging our own furrow. Now we are the Disciples of the One, the Faithful who will bring down the Star of the Empyrean to walk among us and guide us to a glory-filled future. We set ourselves shoulder to shoulder, sharing the burden and the labour equally, charting the course that will reward all, not some.'

Nairo realised he had tears coursing down his cheeks. Through their distortion he could see hundreds in the square below on their knees, foreheads pressed to the unyielding cobbles in supplication. Others had arms raised in tribute, weeping and crying. Lorgar's voice carried over all of this without need for amplification, the raw touch of it enough to set the senses alight, to fill the mind with dreams and faith and strength. Nairo resisted the urge to fall supine in the presence of such holy grandeur, knowing that decorum and restraint were required on such an occasion. He would not embarrass his saviour with such fawning.

3 1 4

Kor Phaeron had set his face in determined passivity from the outset but it was a torture not to grin, not to share the pride and elation he felt as he stood on the balcony above the converts of the One and received their adulation. He knew in an objective part of his brain that their praises were for Lorgar; he was the sun from which all light sprang. But such was the Bearer of the Word's manner, it seemed its power fell only upon those around him.

Cold, cynical politics and manipulation, and no small amount of hidden and bloody work from the Dark Heart had got them to this point. All of that was forgotten in the moment. Kor Phaeron was swept up in the majesty of the occasion, despite his austere exterior.

'This is not the end but the beginning,' Lorgar continued. 'The great works must continue, for the One shall not descend among the unworthy. The old edifices of tyranny and falsehood shall be cast down, replaced with a vision of hope and justice. The Truth incarnate will be made in Vharadesh.'

The thought warmed Kor Phaeron's heart further. He had a vision of the Holy City reborn, its image created afresh to laud not the ancient dirges of the Covenant but the Truth of Kor Phaeron and Lorgar. It was thus daydreaming that Lorgar's next words caught him unaware.

'And the city shall not be the end. All of Colchis must revel in the light of the One,' declared the Ecclesiarch. 'I shall not sit upon a golden throne like an idol to be adored, but shall continue to carry forth the message the One has set into my soul. I shall be the Bearer of the Word still, to bring the Truth to the other cities of Colchis. Such shall be the task of all, whether they walk beside me in the sun or labour alone in the darkness of the deepest cellar of the city. All thought and effort must be turned to the cause of the Truth if we are to receive the benediction and presence of the Star of the Empyrean.

'And when all of Colchis is faithful to the One and the Truth, when as a single world and a single people we raise our voices in prayer together, that shall be the call that brings the One to us.'

3 1 5

It was a struggle for Kor Phaeron to keep in check his anger as they withdrew to the chamber beyond the balcony. The hierarchs of the Covenant were present, along with other assorted clergy and lay staff, and he dared not raise his voice against the Ecclesiarch even though he felt like taking up one of the many gilded ornaments in the reliquary and dashing it across the side of Lorgar's head.

'We did not speak of this,' said the archdeacon, moderating

his tone as much as he could, though the words came out as a terse challenge.

'What do you mean?' replied Lorgar. 'It has always been our mission to bring the Truth to the whole of Colchis. Now that the Covenant lends its might to our cause there is no force on this planet that can resist the Will of the One.'

'You have...' Kor Phaeron grasped for the correct words, mindful not to cause insult in front of witnesses. 'Your words are tantamount to a declaration of war against the other cities. The Covenant's reach spreads far but we do not have the resources to fight all others.'

'There is no cause to speak of war and fighting,' said Lorgar. 'When we came to the gates of Vharadesh were we not welcomed with open arms? Has not the Truth preceded our travels and opened doors and hearts?'

Kor Phaeron swallowed hard, unsure whether Lorgar genuinely believed what he said or was simply trying to manoeuvre him into an impossible position. The archdeacon decided it was the former, for Lorgar was many things but guileful was not one of them. His faith, his genuine belief that there was One who would come to save Colchis, was an affront to the Powers. To speak of it unsettled Kor Phaeron but he had been willing to pay lip service to the idea whilst it gave him the opportunity to destroy his enemies in the Covenant. Now... Now Lorgar spoke of turning the whole world against the Powers with this new religion.

The archdeacon looked at the other priests, saw the fervour in their gazes as they looked upon the Bearer of the Word.

There could be no overt resistance against this new faith. Whatever Lorgar's disposition towards Kor Phaeron, the rest of the priesthood would oust the archdeacon without a second thought, save that cabal of individuals loyal to the plans of Kor Phaeron known with some grim humour as the Dark Heart.

When the war against the cities came, and it would come, Lorgar would be forced to turn to the Powers that had sent him to this world, to beg forgiveness and for their aid. Then Kor Phaeron would ensure that all was ready for the return to the genuine Truth.

And if Lorgar wished to Bear the Word to the rest of Colchis, Kor Phaeron would remain in Vharadesh to attend to the business of the Covenant in the absence of the Ecclesiarch. Had he not railed against the structures and strictures of the old church, the bonds of its outmoded rituals and conformity? Now he had a leader who was willing to proselytise with the same vehemence that had set Kor Phaeron onto this journey, a high priest worthy of the office.

'As you will it, Ecclesiarch,' he said, bowing to Lorgar. He pointed to the ceremonial sceptre carried by the head of the Covenant: a golden, jewelled counterpart to the crude weapon he had fashioned for himself from a censer and axle. He spoke to Lorgar but cast his gaze at the other priests present, making it clear that they too would be venturing forth on this crusade. 'The Faithful shall not be complacent. They shall bring the message of the One to the cities of Colchis. A simple choice that all must face. Submit to the Word of Lorgar, or be crushed beneath the Mace of Lorgar...'

3 2 1

Preparations were well under way for the Faithful to leave Vharadesh to take the Law and Lore of the One to the ignorant cities of Colchis. Four days had passed since Lorgar's inaugural proclamation and the city's efforts had been bent to the creation of the vast enterprise.

Nairo helped marshal the grand expedition, part caravan, part army. Former slaves laboured willingly at the same tasks that years before they had been forced to perform at the end of the scourge. To serve Lorgar was to be part of the coming of the One, a player in the unfolding drama of Colchis' salvation.

Nairo felt it too. Though he was not so often in Lorgar's presence of late, the Ecclesiarch being occupied with his studies and works, Nairo was still filled with the same hope that had stirred him when the child had been found in the camp of the Declined. The liberation of Colchis had begun and would not be stopped. It made him almost tearful to think that he might live to see the day when all on his world were free of bondage, that the dream he had taught others in his youth might become a reality by the hand of Lorgar.

But all was not perfect. Kor Phaeron continued to have his

venomous claws deep in the soul of the Bearer of the Word. The rest-eve before the vanguard of the Faithful host was due to set out, Nairo found himself attending alone to the Ecclesiarch. As he helped the giant man to dress for the final mass – so different from the boy in the desert yet so much the same also – Nairo dared voice his opinion.

'Kor Phaeron has too much power, Bearer of the Word,' he said gently as he slipped a broad belt around the waist of Lorgar. 'You have given him the authority to run all of Vharadesh in your absence.'

'He is my archdeacon,' Lorgar replied, holding up his arms for Nairo to wind the sash about him.

'Always he has served himself as much as you,' Nairo insisted.

'And you have not?' Lorgar said quietly. 'Was it for the One that you followed, or for the chance to be lifted from slavery? I remember the lessons that fell from your lips, equal in machination to the sermons of Kor Phaeron.'

Nairo tied the belt and started to pin golden badges upon the breast of the Ecclesiarch's robe – sigils of his office and the One.

'If that is the case then I have been vindicated, for the freeing of those in serfdom has paved the way to the glorious ascent of the One.' He slid plain silver rings onto the massive fingers of his holy master. 'Kor Phaeron is archdeacon, but in your absence might as well be Ecclesiarch. What tempers his ambition now?'

'What more could he achieve?' countered Lorgar. 'If, as you say, he is paramount in authority, he aspires only to maintain such position. Above all else he is still driven by the True Word, and in me he has seen that given form, and through me has been delivered to the heights from which the Truth shall be spread. Even if self-interest should guide him, it is married to the interests of the Covenant and the One.'

* * *

3 2 2

Nairo found he could not argue against this, though half-formed misgivings still nagged him when he returned to his chambers, his sleep that night fitful, his dreams portending some formless disaster yet to come. He woke fatigued. The former slave performed his final tasks in a half-sleep until he and a mass of others were assembled outside the city.

Soldiers and riders numbered in their thousands, accompanied by such engines and vehicles as could be made available – wagons and half-tracks, armoured trucks and sun-yachts in their hundreds. With them, shaded by great parasols carried by teams of sternbacks, the Faithful waited for the Ecclesiarch. Priests and deacons of all ranks, along with countless missionaries and freed slaves, with food stockpiled over the preceding days, great tankers of water and feed for the beasts drawn by teams of hundreds. Manpower was not an issue for the Covenant – there were countless multitudes willing to bend their backs and blister their hands in service to the Bearer of the Word, in exchange for a blessing or just to be in the presence of the Golden One.

Lorgar appeared at the gate and the cheer of the Faithful shook the walls – walls recently repaired and bolstered, which spoke something of Kor Phaeron's paranoia that all would not go well and enemies might come to Vharadesh sooner rather than later. As large as the force that departed was, ten thousand armed followers still remained to guard the City of Grey Flowers against an enemy that might think to strike at the Covenant's heart while its spiritual leader was abroad.

With the Ecclesiarch came his archdeacon, carried upon a shade-covered sedan chair in the burgeoning light of Dawnaway. Lorgar walked beside it, unheeding of the sun's merciless power. Kor Phaeron stepped down and Nairo was close enough to hear the exchange between them.

'Go with the blessings of the Covenant as well as its mortal servants,' said Kor Phaeron.

Voice trembling, Lorgar laid a hand upon the back of Kor Phaeron's head and bowed, touching his forehead to that of the man who had raised him as his son and acolyte.

'Be strong for me, father, and stand ready for my call.'

'All that you need, Vharadesh shall provide,' Kor Phaeron assured him.

'I shall not return to these gates until Colchis is saved,' promised Lorgar. He straightened, nodded gently as though assuring himself, and set his eyes upon the distant horizon. He raised his voice so that it carried across the vast tumult of humanity sprawled before the Holy City, his words carried to the minds and hearts of all who were present within and without.

'It begins! The Word or the Mace shall be our creed. We must be merciful but unflinching, compassionate yet relentless. Every life lost in the cause shall be in vain if we shirk from the final duty the One has set before us, yet each soul saved shall live immortal in the Empyrean of the One. We may falter, we may fall, but we cannot be defeated while we stay faithful to the Truth. Onwards, children of the One, onwards to glory and salvation!'

3 2 3

As Lorgar had spoken, so it was.

Great were his accomplishments, and sparse is the time and space for their recollection. Be it known that he travelled and laboured for many days along the coast and into the deserts, bringing the Word and the Truth with him.

The Faithful first came upon Golgora, beyond the Covenant city of Tezenesh, and before the walls Lorgar spoke of the Truth and the coming of the One. The viziers and elders of Golgora had not been idle in the time of Lorgar's ascension, and knew well of the Bearer of the Word and the following he had gathered. Touched by the spirit of the One they opened their gates to the Faithful as had Vharadesh, and welcomed the Truth into their city.

So it was at Ctholl and Martias, Lanansa and Hourldesh. Yet not every city was pleased to be subjected to enlightenment. At Epicea, for long centuries a stronghold of the Church of the Archivist Deliverance, boulders were cast from catapults on the walls and flaming arrows welcomed the disciples of the Truth.

Mighty were reckoned the towers of that city, yet for only a Long Noon, Post-noon and Duskeve did they hold against the fervour of the Faithful. Assailed from without, finally the city was broken from within by those who had been swayed to the Truth brought to them by the words of Lorgar. At the fall, as Lorgar had promised, the Epiceans were given the choice of submission or death. A few chose death and were quickly sent to the Empyrean to meet the judgement of the One. Most chose conversion, either out of fear or finally repenting before the sermon of the Ecclesiarch, having initially resisted out of fear of slavery. Knowing that they would be able to live freely under the Covenant, where before they would have faced subjugation, the Epiceans rejoiced for a whole day and wholeheartedly swore their city to the cause.

Other cities resisted or capitulated, or were razed, their populations slain to the last adult, irrevocably corrupted by their wayward faith and dogma. Great was the carnage at Cathrace, where only one in ten converted, and tears marked the cheeks of the Ecclesiarch as the great pyres consumed the bodies of those who refused to hear the Truth.

Nairo watched his holy master mourn the city from Duskeve to Coldfall two days after, as he went alone into the desert to seek solace and communion with the One, returning with a shroud over his face and his golden skin hidden beneath the ash of the razed city.

3 3 1

Many were sent to Vharadesh, not in captivity but as pilgrims ready to learn. They were set to labour for the Covenant, as willing servants not as slaves, building roads and stations, digging canals and founding convents and monasteries upon the route to guide the Faithful back to the Holy City.

From among these converts, thousands were sent forth upon long journeys across the desert, or by ship around the vast coast of the continent. They were tasked by Kor Phaeron to move ahead of the host of Lorgar, to those cities where opposition was yet strong. By word and deed they weakened the resolve of the defenders, sometimes even conducting a coup or otherwise overthrowing the city before the Faithful had actually arrived.

Among the upper hierarchy of Vharadesh these clandestine missionaries and warriors were known as the *ushmetar kaul* – 'the blade that cuts mortal existence to part the way to the Empyrean mount'. They more frequently called themselves the Brotherhood of the Knife.

As the Word spread across the continent, along the coasts and up the scant rivers, so the network, prosperity and civilisation of the City of Grey Flowers grew, sending tribute and people in ever-growing numbers to the coffers and cloisters of the archdeacon.

Kor Phaeron oversaw this vast swelling of temporal power, hordes of converts sent to him by Lorgar inculcated into the beliefs of the Covenant, as appropriately directed by the archdeacon and his coterie of hierarchs. Never did he stray from the Word of Lorgar, yet as well as the Ecclesiarch's teachings he impressed upon the newly Faithful the need for obedience and discipline, the virtues of sacrifice and the necessity of determination.

Thus moulded, armed and trained, these Faithful were dispatched back across the deserts to return their strength to the host of Lorgar so that for every servant to the One who fell conquering the recalcitrant, ten more eventually took their place.

After nearly a whole turn about the sun of Colchis, near four years as the Terran adepts measure such things, the host of Lorgar was numbered in the hundreds of thousands. Mere rumour of their approach was enough to bring the surrender of all but the most zealously irreligious. Cities purged of the irredeemable were founded anew in the image of Vharadesh, where academies and seminaries staffed by Kor Phaeron's chosen continued to promulgate the message of the Covenant further and further.

Missionaries moved even further afield into the deserts, bringing the Word of the Wyrmslayer to the tribes of the inner wastes, so that there was not a civilised person nor nomad upon the great continent who had not heard the name of Lorgar. The matriarchs of Tezenesh even dubbed Lorgar 'the Urizen', meaning the wisest of the wise, the Architect of Faith – a prophetic and loaded title that had only previously been held, legend claimed, by the Prophet Tezen himself.

* * *

On more than one occasion the Ecclesiarch voiced his confessions and doubts to Nairo, who became his confidante in the absence of Kor Phaeron, and witnessed the debilitation and exultation of Lorgar's visions. With each city that fell it seemed that the Ecclesiarch became both more determined and sickened by what he had unleashed. More fervent became his pleas to those who resisted, though the army at his back bayed for the blood of unbelievers and blasphemers.

Several times splinter armies, led by overzealous gun-deacons or just wayward followers beset by the need to prove their faith, attacked wantonly, besieging and sacking towns and cities without the prior knowledge or authority of Lorgar.

Nairo suspected the hand of Kor Phaeron in some of these pre-emptive assaults, for the archdeacon had always had a thirst for physical chastisement. If the effect had been intended to cow all resistance with these shows of force, the consequence was the opposite. Resistance to the rule of the Covenant hardened against Lorgar. Where at first some may have believed the Covenant not able to reach across the continent to them, the continued expansions and conversion of city after city threatened all.

Nairo told Lorgar to sanction these offenders, but the Ecclesiarch could not chastise them for unruly faith – only make it known that he was displeased with any life taken without effort to convert beforehand.

Coalitions between the remaining cities formed against the Bearer of the Word, yet none could match either the oratory or the military power of Lorgar. The Ecclesiarch himself was worth an army of mortal soldiers, at the forefront of every attack bellowing his prayers to the One even as he smote those who would defy him. Not on Colchis was born the warrior who could match him face to face, nor the demagogue who could quell the power of Lorgar's voice. Such had become his skill with languages and linguistics, the Ecclesiarch needed only to spend a day in the presence of a native, or to read a handful of the texts of the faithless, to understand their idioms and beliefs, their culture and morals. There was not a dialect or theological argument he could not overcome, and by such means even as his armies tore down walls and keeps, his words broke open entire denominations and belief systems. Sermonised in their own tongue, many were the potential foes persuaded to convert by this fact alone.

Even those who had been raised in abject hatred of all that came from Vharadesh were reduced to tears and prayers when subjected to the love and testimony of the Bearer of the Word. Salvation at the hands of the One, acknowledgement of the benighted centuries that had beset Colchis, freed many from the shackles of disbelief that had held their opinion against the Holy City.

Nairo saw Lorgar grieve for every life ended. Sometimes ten thousand or twenty thousand of the Faithful were sacrificed against the defences of the unholy, yet he remembered them in his speeches and his dreams were haunted by their deaths.

'The price of the Truth,' he would tell Nairo with anguish, 'is too high.'

Then he would order the next attack, knowing that he was set upon a course and to abandon his plan now would render everything undone, a failure to the One and the millions who now looked to him for spiritual guidance and leadership.

3 3 3

Nairo became increasingly worried by Lorgar. The closer the Ecclesiarch came to achieving his goals, the worse it seemed the visions assailed him. He tried his best to shelter Lorgar during these times, when madness and mania threatened and the Ecclesiarch was reduced to a mewling, frothing wreck in his grand pavilion. There were rumours, fiercely quenched by Nairo and others, that some other malaise afflicted the Bearer of the Word, some infection of the deep desert he had contracted – or that the spirit of the Kingwyrm had possessed him in vengeance for its destruction.

His holy master was plagued by them, often through the dark hours of Coldfall, Long Night and Dawnaway, sometimes even longer. Nairo begged Lorgar to return to Vharadesh to seek the aid of the mentalists and physicians of the Holy City, but Lorgar would repeat his vow not to set foot in the City of Grey Flowers while the soul of Colchis remained threatened. Nairo even conspired with Axata to send secret missives to Kor Phaeron, imploring the archdeacon to come forth and see to the welfare of his adopted son. No reply came and Nairo was forced to conclude that Kor Phaeron no longer cared for the well-being of Lorgar.

He did his best to provide such support and succour as he was able, but sometimes terror at what beset his lord unmanned him, sending Nairo scurrying for the shelter of his own companions while unearthly rages and depressions enveloped the Ecclesiarch.

Despite this, or perhaps because of the obvious touch of the One's power upon their leader, the faith of those close to the Ecclesiarch never wavered during these episodes, and neither did Lorgar's. He emerged from each mania and stupor invigorated and enlightened, and made fresh proclamations about his beliefs and understanding of the ordering of the Empyrean.

3 3 4

Watching the thousands of dead piled onto the pyres outside the broken wall of Khathage, the sky a pall of black from the corpse fires already burning, Nairo tasted bile in his throat. Every city that had resisted had suffered a similar fate – the cohorts of Axata had stormed the walls and butchered any who gave resistance. Those who laid down their arms, with the young and infirm, were brought before Lorgar to hear the Golden One speak. Few who survived to hear him continued in their faithless ways, but there were always some, buried deep in the blasphemies of their cults, who remained deaf to the truth.

With scarves and masks to shield themselves from the smoke and stench, long columns of the Faithful laboured to pile the bodies on the scrub and sands. Ordained priests walked among them, the fume of their censers lost amongst the charnel smog. They prayed for the souls of the dead to be shown mercy by the One, for they did not understand the trespasses they had performed against the Truth. Even in the Empyrean Lorgar hoped to save their souls from the damnation of faithlessness.

Doused in blessed oil, the timbers of the fresh pyres were lit and greenish-blue flames consumed the last sons and daughters of the Gods Path faith that had held sway over the Khathagians, their remains and spirits carried to the sky among the stench of burned flesh and perfume of thick incense.

Nairo felt movement beside him and a slender Duskeve shadow fell across the grey sand next to his own.

'More infidels for the One,' said Castora.

Always one of the most zealous, even enslaved by Kor Phaeron, the former herald now sported the robes and faux crown of a hierarch. She had prospered under the tutelage and patronage of Lorgar, one of the handful of the original slaves of the caravan who still survived. L'sai had been spitted by a plasma lance at Kuldanesh. Parentha and Koa had both succumbed to sandlung, wasted away as they undertook the long march between Assakhor and Jo Burgesh. Kal Dekka was head of the tutelary that had set up in Nuresh Ab, known after its capitulation as the Repentant City. Lorra had become a gun-deacon, charged with patrolling the highways between Golgora and Vharadesh. Other names and faces crowded Nairo's memories. Hu Osys, the leader of the Taranthians. She had died poorly, trampled during a sternback stampede. Declined tribespeople who had joined during the early months after the arrival of Lorgar, and converts who had flocked to the call of the Wyrmslayer. Most of them, hundreds with names he could not recall, now dead.

Of the guards even fewer remained. Axata, gundeacon-prime under Kor Phaeron. A few others in positions of command, the former converts rewarded with battalions and cohorts to lead. Lorgar seemed not to care about this nepotism, his mind occupied by the 'symphonies of the Empyrean above' – the otherworldly choir that only he could hear.

'Men and women,' Nairo corrected Castora. 'People.'

'Ignorant savages,' said Castora.

'We were ignorant once. The One does not desire sacrifice for its own sake, but in the labour of the One's works.'

'The offering will be well sent, whatever the One desires.' Her exultation diminished as some fresh thought occurred to her.

'What worries you?'

'There is but one city left to bow to the Will of Lorgar.'

'That concerns you, that this bloodletting will be over?' Nairo shook his head. 'I would end this purgation tomorrow.'

'Many more will die before Colchis is united,' warned Castora. 'Gahevarla remains. The City of the Magisters.'

'The Scourstorm,' whispered Nairo. 'Hurricane winds of dust and lightning that rage for days conjured by the rulers of the city. No foe has ever survived to reach the walls of Gahevarla...'

Castora gave him a long look, no words needed to convey her bleak thoughts. Perhaps with good reason Lorgar had avoided confrontation with the magisters before now, yet the fate of the world would turn at Gahevarla, as unavoidable and deadly as the coming of the Long Noon and the freezing High Night.

3 4 1

'Sirash!' Kor Phaeron bellowed again for his aide. 'Sirash, I need more ink!'

He would have the laggard priest flogged for his tardiness, the archdeacon vowed as he returned his attention to the pile of assorted materials on his desk – wafers and parchments, paper and autoscribed sheets, all covered with a plethora of text and handwriting.

'I asked Sirash to step out for a while.'

The voice caused Kor Phaeron's heart to hammer in his chest and he looked up with a gasp, scarce believing he'd heard it.

At the grand doorway into the suite of chambers held by the archdeacon stood a figure swathed in dark hood and robe – an appalling disguise really for one who was nearly twice as tall as a normal man.

'Lorgar!' Kor Phaeron shot to his feet, a flood of competing thoughts racing through his mind. Why had he returned? Was something amiss? Had he learned of Kor Phaeron's 'refugee relocation' activities with some of the survivors of the pro-Powers cults? Was the war over? This last question burned to the top of the list. 'Gahevarla has fallen?'

'Is that the welcome you give me?' Lorgar pulled back his hood to reveal his naked scalp, much tanned by his long travels. 'It has been near a year and a half since I departed these walls. Have you no fondness at all for my return?'

'You are Ecclesiarch, Lorgar, not a wayward child,' chided Kor Phaeron. 'When you departed you swore that you would not return until the One held dominion over all of Colchis. Is that so?'

'Not yet,' confessed Lorgar. He cast about for somewhere to sit, but found nothing equal to his weight and bulk, and so sat on the floor in front of Kor Phaeron's desk, his head still level with the standing archdeacon. Kor Phaeron sat down in his ornate chair, somewhat grateful for the illusion of a barrier his desk provided. There was something different about his former acolyte.

'You have seen much,' he said, drawing his own conclusion. 'The hidden nature of mortals and faith has been revealed to you. You see another Truth.'

'I would not wish what I have witnessed on any mortal.'

'But it was unavoidable. When there is only One, there can be no others. This is fundamental to your faith.'

'Our faith. And I do not swerve from that course.'

'For one so gifted with words and speech, you lie terribly, Lorgar. Your presence betrays a swerve.'

'Not in my faith in the One. The visions are more powerful than ever. It is that which has brought me here. The golden figure and the one-eyed magister. What if it is a warning. Gahevarla is protected by arcane technosorceries. What if the magister I see in my dreams is one of them? Am I to make alliance not conquest?'

'Have they shown themselves willing to listen to the Word?'

'For a quarter of a year the Scourstorm has raged. None have entered or left Gahevarla in that time. I do not think they wish to parley.'

'The very stones of the city are steeped in the blood of sacrifices to the Powers, as much as the Holy City. Are you willing to share authority with those who would continue to rip the hearts from their servants, to offer up the burned remains of their foes to the lords of the Empyrean?'

'That is not the Lore and the Law of the One.'

'And there is your answer, Lorgar. You have travelled for many days for nothing. As with all matters of faith, you had your answer already. Or was it something else that you wanted to share?'

3 4 2

Lorgar did not answer, but stood and paced for a while, head almost brushing the great chandeliers that hung from the dome of the office. Though his attention was elsewhere, Kor Phaeron did not think he was listening to the universal music that filled his thoughts.

'What are you writing?' Lorgar asked suddenly, ignoring the archdeacon's earlier question.

'Transcribing,' Kor Phaeron replied. He indicated the scraps and ragtag documents. 'Your words, actually. There are different versions all over Colchis, from every converted city and tribe and pilgrimage. Records of your sermons, transcripts of your conversations with converts and foes alike. Your story, your faith and your thoughts given form.'

'Edited appropriately?' suggested Lorgar. Kor Phaeron felt himself flush at the gentle accusation, but could not deny it.

'Only for brevity and clarity. You repeat yourself often. I will show it to no other until you have approved my work.'

Lorgar nodded absentmindedly, not quite comprehending the importance of Kor Phaeron's literary endeavour.

'It is to replace the *Revelations of the Prophets.*'

This cold statement sank into Lorgar's thoughts and a fierce light burned in his eyes.

'You worried once that I might be the Prophet of the Fifth Power, but I am more than that. I am the cleansing, the purification of Colchis. All blasphemies shall be washed away to prepare for the arrival of the One.'

Kor Phaeron let nothing of his unease show, though unseen beneath the desk his fingers made a swift sign of the Four, a brief assurance to the Powers that one of true faith remained and would return Colchis to them.

'So now you have found that which you needed to confront the magisters?'

'I have,' said Lorgar with a smile, but it soon faded and was replaced by an expression of fatigue. He looked through the door to the neighbouring bedchamber and its grand cot. 'Might I prevail upon your hospitality for rest-eve? I shall leave Vharadesh with the first light of Mornday to be back with my army by Dawnaway.'

The archdeacon nodded, wondering how the Ecclesiarch might cross a continent so swiftly.

Lorgar ducked through the archway. It was only a matter of moments before the sonorous breathing of the giant sounded from the adjoining room. Kor Phaeron moved to the communications chamber, past the artifices that linked to the prayer-hailers in temples across the city, and opened the shutters to step out onto the balcony. Here trained messenger ravens were kept in an aviary, as sure a method of contact as the temperamental archeotech that the gun-deacons used to communicate over long distances.

He retrieved a small slip of paper from a receptacle beside the cage and the pen beside it, and wrote quickly. Opening the aviary, he selected a bird and slid the message into the tube on its leg. He released the raven, which swiftly disappeared into the night, heading for the waystation at Ouralto, and from there via other means to Silena.

For good or ill, Lorgar's fate would be determined in the coming days, and with it the future of the Covenant. It was time for the Dark Heart to assemble and prepare for either eventuality.

3 5 1

Nairo watched with trepidation, his hands sweating despite the chill of Dawnaway. The lamps of vehicles cut through the twilight and the sea of lanterns carried by the cohorts of Axata manoeuvred across the wastes in pre-planned circuits and lines. Behind the former slave the camp was already alight and alive with other preparations, but the mood was uncertain. Nobody had seen Lorgar for the previous day, and Axata had been tight-lipped about their holy master's whereabouts and intentions. For all that Nairo knew, the Ecclesiarch was still in his pavilion writing and studying, or perhaps communing with the One in preparation for the coming assault.

If he knew Lorgar, and he believed he did better than anyone, the Bearer of the Word was deep in contemplation of the carnage that was about to ensue from his next command.

His attention was drawn to a movement at the far edge of the camp. People were surging from the mess tents and ablution quarters, abandoning their morning rituals as they crowded down the tented streets, the disturbance passing through the camp-city like a ripple. Shouts rang out, growing in volume, further clamour from bells and gongs added to the increasing noise.

Nairo saw others nearby running from their tents and demanded to know what was happening.

'The Golden One!' someone shouted. 'He has returned from the desert.'

Nairo found himself running too, and was soon drawn into a huge crowd surging through the camp in the direction of Lorgar's approach. He called to several guards looking dumbfounded at this mass, demanding that they act as escort for him. Though never ordained, Nairo was regarded as a talisman of the One, a mascot almost, and all knew him. Their attention called to his presence by the voices of the ward-adepts, the Faithful did their best to part at his approach. Even so it took some time for him to make his way through the press of people to see what was happening.

Lorgar had emerged from the darkness and was on the edge of the camp, surrounded by his followers. Though they did their best to keep a respectful distance, gun-deacons and rod bearers holding back the living wall, the pressure of so many people created an ever-constricting circle around the Ecclesiarch.

Those amongst the Faithful who were close enough to be seen waved prayer books and sheaves of their own writings – or copies of Lorgar's sermons that acted as a secondary scrip among the servants and soldiers of the camp, so valued were his words. They called for the blessings of the One, and where the violet gaze of the Ecclesiarch fell there was much crying out, swooning and declarations of undying faith. Some afflicted with the sandlung and bone-cankers called out to be healed by the power of the single divinity of Colchis.

Slowly the bubble around Lorgar moved with him, opening in the crowd, until he spied Nairo amongst the throng, alert to every detail as ever. He beckoned for Nairo to approach but his invitation was misunderstood and a woman with a babe beside the former teacher ran forwards and fell to her knees, offering up her son as though a gift to Lorgar.

'Golden One, lay thy hands upon my son – may he be blessed in the gaze of the One.'

'He is already blessed by a mother of faith,' Lorgar replied with a smile.

Nairo saw something in the gaze he had not witnessed before. Where he had known only humility and concern, now in the eyes of Lorgar he saw triumph, as though the adulation of the crowd was already a victory. He could only guess at what had occurred during Lorgar's absence, but he knew he did not like the sight.

3 5 2

'I don't think they're listening.'

Axata's attempt at humour was poorly received by the hierarchs and gun-deacons who accompanied Lorgar. Half a kilometre ahead of them the desert seemed to churn and boil, rising straight up into a shifting wall of debris and crackling energy. The tempest field of Gahevarla.

It extended far into the sky, blotting out the early sun so that the host of Lorgar waited in an unnatural, shifting umbra. Such shade would have been gratefully received under other circumstances, but its presence left a clammy chill upon Nairo. The only sound was the crackle of energy and the hiss of sand particles slashing the air.

The former slave tightened his grip on the haft of his powered maul. He had never used it for its true purpose, having been happy to remain towards the back of the cohorts behind the more aggressive – and frankly more skilled – members of Lorgar's millions-strong congregation. Hanging back would not spare him the tribulations of this battle, though. There was only one route to Gahevarla and it lay directly though the Scourstorm.

A gun wagon clad in thick plates of iron, studded with rivets and heavily welded, ventured forwards at a signal from Axata. It had not even reached the periphery of the storm when a bolt of lightning flared from the undulating field, arcing several metres to earth through the fuel store. Vapour detonated with an explosion that jolted everyone present save Lorgar, scattering metal and body parts over forty metres of scorched earth.

Everyone's mood soured even further at the thought of marching through the storm on foot.

Nairo looked over his shoulder. Thirty thousand gun-deacons, armed acolytes, sword-adepts and warrior priests stood ready to advance. It was likely that not one of them would make it to the walls of Gahevarla, their broken bodies scattered to the Empyrean on the devil-winds of the magisters.

'Waiting won't make it easier,' Axata declared. He took a step towards the land yacht not far away, where his staff of officers waited. 'Might as well give the order.'

He had taken three more strides when Lorgar's quiet command halted him.

'Wait.'

3 5 3

The single word stopped everybody. Nairo's breath caught in his throat, almost choking him.

Relaxed, seemingly entirely at ease with the world, Lorgar broke from his followers and advanced towards the storm. Nairo wanted to call out, to warn him that even his One-blessed frame and constitution could not withstand the assault of the

Scourstorm. His flesh would be shriven from his skeleton and all would be failure.

The words caught the same as his breath and remained unsaid. The agitation of the others around him testified that they were similarly afflicted as they watched the holy master walk to his doom.

Just ten metres from the wall of furious elements he stopped. Lorgar seemed to consider the Scourstorm for some time, marshalling his thoughts.

He knelt, head bowed to the sands, the touch of the outer winds lifting particles across his head, settling drifts of sand in the folds of his robes. He remained motionless for some time.

Words drifted on the wind. Praises to the One. Nairo heard scattered mention of the names of cities – settlements that had been brought into the dominion of the Covenant. Other testimony was made, of dedication and faith.

And finally, an invocation. Not a prayer, not a request.

A demand.

'The Powers desired death to sate their appetites, to pay for their gifts. I have told these people that the Lore and the Law of the One is different. A life lost in earnest endeavour shall be remarked, but it is our labours that we sacrifice, not our existence. Heed me not and I will still give the order. I will lead these people myself into the uncaring storm. It will take me and Colchis will never be yours. I do not ask this of you, I do not threaten you, I simply state what shall be if you desire it.'

He stood up, mace in one hand, the very same weapon he had fashioned to slay the convert mutineers years before, though much reinforced with bands of metal and studs.

Lorgar started walking again and fronds of power leapt from the storm, coruscating across his golden skin, earthing along his limbs.

* * *

3 5 4

The wall of the Scourstorm bowed before Lorgar's advance, opening up as if to embrace him even as lightning of green and purple and white flared and spat around the Ecclesiarch.

He lifted his arms and the breach widened as though at his command. Churning sand parted, forming a ravine of moving rocks and swirling grit to either side, bridges of power crackling across the growing divide. Into this breach advanced Lorgar.

'Move!' Axata bellowed, racing to his yacht. 'All cohorts advance!'

The command was broadcast on hailer and hidden wave, and within moments the host of Lorgar started to march. Armoured rigs and multi-turreted gun wagons prowled forwards among their ranks.

The sand shifted beneath Nairo's feet and he found himself stumbling forwards, moving into the chasm of the storm as though into a waiting maw. Not since his near death beneath the millicrawler had he felt the presence of the One so keenly. His nerves sang with the divine presence, ears pounding, heart racing as he followed Lorgar into the dark canyon.

3 5 5

Gahevarla fell by the end of Long Noon.

Led by Lorgar, the host of the Faithful took the walls by rest-eve of Mornday. Relentless, they poured into the city and the central citadel was besieged by the coming of wake-main on Long Noon. The last of the magisters held out from the tower and cast bolts of black energy and a fog of toxic green vapour into the horde of the faithful, slaying hundreds, until Lorgar himself shattered the gates of their inner keep. The sorcerer died by Axata's hand even as the hot winds blew away the remnants of the Scourstorm.

Upon a barbican of the keep Lorgar stood with Nairo and Axata, while in the streets of the city below the process of conversion continued apace, priests moving amongst the shocked inhabitants preaching the Truth of the One.

'So that's done then,' said Axata. He sighed, his relief evident.

Lorgar remained silent.

'All of Colchis is united beneath the Book and the Flame,' said Nairo, in reference to the sigil of the Covenant. There had been a time when such a declaration, the thought of a single unified church controlling the lives of every person on the planet would have filled him with horror. With Lorgar at the head of that church it seemed the most natural, beautiful thing beneath the Empyrean.

Lorgar said nothing.

'There'll still be a few malcontents, always is,' said Axata. He glanced past the broad chest of the Ecclesiarch to meet Nairo's gaze, concern written on his features. 'But we've won. It's over. Time to celebrate.'

Still Lorgar stared into the distance without response.

Nairo thought him in the grip of a vision, but there was none of the pain or elation matched with such an occurrence, so he was forced to conclude that his holy master was simply so deep in thought he did not hear them. He motioned for himself and Axata to depart, but as the two of them turned to head towards the steps from the rampart Lorgar finally spoke.

'This is not the end,' he said slowly. 'It is simply the conclusion of the beginning.'

3 6 1

The pealing of bells, the chimes and gongs of a hundred temples drowned out the roars and cheers of the millions-strong crowd that thronged the approaches through Vharadesh. Already swelled by years of refugees and converts, the city had passed its walls like a lake breaking its banks. Vast suburbs had been erected and about these new constructions a shanty-camp every bit as large as the City of Grey Flowers spread into the deserts, populated by a massive influx of pilgrims in anticipation of Lorgar's glorious return.

The Ecclesiarch rode upon the pulpit of a gilded temple-rig – the same truck that had carried him in the deserts with Kor Phaeron years before, now engineered and bedecked with the finest the Covenant could offer. On the cab rode Axata, and beside him Nairo and others who were hailed as the First Disciples, the Heralds of the One.

Nairo despised such monikers, thought them an affront to his ideals of equality, but Lorgar said to pay them no mind, an affectation that would soon fade as Colchis passed into a true age of enlightenment.

As they moved through the tents and caravans and into the city proper, Nairo was shocked by what he saw. When he had left the main thoroughfares had been lined with shrines and schools, monasteries of different sects and disciplines. Winding alleys and narrow souks had played home to throngs of worshippers and preachers.

All revels had been forced out of the city, so that an austere, respectful quiet greeted them. The streets were lined with the ordained, priest and deacon alike, heads bowed slightly in respect for their returning hero.

Much had been levelled. The academy where he had taught was now a broad plaza, tiled with gold and silver. Mosaic icons of the One decorated the walls of buildings, standing where temples and ossuaries had been demolished and rebuilt, literally reshaped in the new image of the Covenant.

And statues. Statues everywhere, of Kor Phaeron and Lorgar. In marble and granite, gold and silver, of alabaster and painted limestone, it seemed there was not a square, marketplace or processional that was not beneath the gaze of one of these life-sized – sometimes even larger – idols.

The Spire Temple loomed over all, much refurbished and redecorated, though its grand tower was dominant as ever, a finger thrust towards the Godpeak of the Empyrean. Broad steps led from the plaza before the temple to an arched portico thirty metres high.

A solitary figure waited on the white stair for them.

Kor Phaeron.

3 6 2

At the approach of his Ecclesiarch, Kor Phaeron lowered to one knee, hands clasped to his chest, chin bowed. He remained thus only for a few heartbeats before straightening. Flanked by Axata and Nairo, Lorgar ascended.

The archdeacon had not thought it possible. Not when Lorgar had first declared his intent to bring all of Colchis into the fold of the Covenant. Kor Phaeron chided himself for his lack of ambition in that regard, and his doubts. The Ecclesiarch had proven himself more than capable and now as archdeacon, Kor Phaeron ruled a world.

He had set in motion plans to ensure his continued pre-eminence, but Lorgar's success at Gahevarla cemented Kor Phaeron's position more than anything. The people would worship Lorgar as they worshipped the One. Let him be the figurehead; it was not the praise that Kor Phaeron desired.

The church was his, the world his. All were sworn to his service, in reality if not word.

Kor Phaeron smiled.

'Welcome home, your holy majesty.'

3 6 3

Lorgar did not return the smile.

'There is still much to be done,' said the Ecclesiarch.

'Of course,' said Kor Phaeron. 'Those cities still fresh to the cause have not yet been fully embraced by the Covenant, but missions are already under way.'

'It is not that.' Lorgar looked across the city, distracted for a moment. 'A very fine place you have made. A jewel, and all our cities shall be fashioned likewise. But news of victory is misplaced.'

'I heard that Gahevarla no longer kneels beneath the yoke of the magisters. Was that wrong?'

'The magisters are gone,' confirmed Lorgar. He glanced at Nairo and Axata before continuing, 'I have heard that all is not as it appears.'

Kor Phaeron feigned ignorance, though he knew the rapid

beating of his heart was audible to the remarkable man before him. The Ecclesiarch continued, not seeming to notice this sudden panicked reaction.

'Beneath the masquerade of the Covenant there are sects and cults still dedicated to the Powers. And even among those who acknowledge the authority of the One, some have begun to speak out against rule from Vharadesh. Against me. The work, my sermons, is it finished?'

'Yes. The new book for the Faithful is ready to approve, Ecclesiarch.'

'It shall be the cornerstone of our new order. All shall learn the Truth from its words. There must be no dissent. Only in utter unity shall we bring forth the One from the Empyrean.'

'Then we shall purge the taint,' said Kor Phaeron. 'No heretic will be left alive to move against your will.'

'Yes, ' said Lorgar. 'A purge.'

3 6 4

'Of ideas,' Nairo said hurriedly. 'We shall teach the Truth, with this book of which you speak.'

The thought of more bloodshed filled him with grim terror, not least for his own well-being. Even more so, the idea that the millions who had already died were not enough blood to sate Kor Phaeron's thirst for power and revenge sickened him to the core. The archdeacon could not be allowed to dictate the thoughts of Lorgar in this matter.

'It was from slavery that you led us, holy master,' Nairo said, wringing his hands. 'Freedom, not subjugation, is the Lore and the Law. It matters not if it is the hand of the Ecclesiarch or his words that are laid upon them – men and women must be free to speak their mind. The Word, not the Mace.'

'Nonsense,' rasped Kor Phaeron. 'Opposition must be crushed without delay. It is a canker, a rot that will destroy all we have built from within. A brotherhood stands ready to serve your will.'

Lorgar looked between his two companions, Axata having withdrawn slightly, feeling out of place in such a debate.

'You two shall never be in accord. Shall you make me umpire and peacekeeper for evermore?'

'This witless slave would have you throw away everything, make a mockery of all who have given their lives, given limbs and health for you. You cannot let this wretch soil your thoughts with his cowardly counsel any longer.'

'Kor Phaeron has used you from the moment he killed those who saved you in the desert,' Nairo replied hotly. 'Can you not see? He beat and whipped you into subservience, and though you wear the grey of Ecclesiarch he has made himself master. He has filled your head with nothing but his poison, and now he would turn you into his enforcer, a glorified cult thug.'

Lorgar's brow creased at this accusation and he looked at Kor Phaeron.

'Filthy lies!' shrieked Kor Phaeron.

Nairo did not see the fist that caught his chin and before he realised that the archdeacon had struck he tumbled down several steps, bruising ribs and elbows. He did not rightly know what he did, but realised that his dagger, which for a year had remained in its sheath at his hip, was now in his hand.

3 6 5

Kor Phaeron stared in shock, time slowing as Nairo launched himself up the steps, knife aimed for the archdeacon. He started to raise a hand to ineffectually ward off the blow, disgusted with himself for letting the slave rise so high in the opinions of Lorgar.

It was a stupid, filthy way to die.

A shadow covered him when Lorgar moved. Kor Phaeron saw the head of the mace, once the censer that had spilled incense through the masses of his caravan. It descended like a comet trailing gilded chains and talismans, and connected with Nairo's head.

The slave's skull split asunder and his shoulder shattered beneath the blow, spine crumpling into ruin under the weight of it. The tip of the knife nicked Kor Phaeron's chin as it flew from lifeless fingers.

Nairo folded into himself, crushed against the steps, legs snapping as his torso was driven down by the hammer blow of a demigod.

Choking back a cry, Kor Phaeron stepped backwards, equally terrified and elated by the look that burned in the gaze of Lorgar. The Golden One, the Bearer of the Word, Urizen Ecclesiarch of the Covenant stood with hands bloodied, Nairo's corpse at his feet. A nimbus of gold seemed to play about his head, though it may have simply been reflected sunlight.

Lorgar lifted up a gore-covered finger and pointed to the skies.

'He is coming!' he declared. 'We shall be ready!'

THE GALAXY BURNS

964.M40

Forty-Seven One (formerly Karlstadt)

It was fitting that it ended where it had begun. Almost. Birthed on Colchis, upon a balcony of the Spire Temple, Lorgar's mission to spread the word of the Emperor first became a reality among the stars on this planet.

Kor Phaeron remembered the elation of the primarch, his zeal unleashed upon a waiting galaxy by the arrival of the Emperor and Magnus, gifted a Legion of superhuman warriors and the population of Colchis to further his *magnum deus.*

Karlstadt had been an easy compliance, in comparison to some. The Golden One had approached the compliance of a world the same way he had viewed the conversion of a city-state of Colchis. One offered the Word and if it was not accepted, delivered the Mace. His first planetary conquest had required both; the broadcasts of the Urizen had ignited the fires of worship among some of the planetary nations, who in turn received military assistance from the XVII Legion to destroy their enemies.

This was the very place where Lorgar had made planetfall,

the mount upon which he had raised the first Grand Cathedral of the Saviour Delivered.

The temple was vast, encompassing much of the summit of the mountain from which it had been dug and built, nearly three kilometres long. The main nave ran for a third of that length, and within the vast structure had been assembled the commanders and their staffs from every Chapter of the Legion. Scores of captains and Chaplains, the banners of their companies with them, watched from afar by the golden-armoured Custodians sent to enforce the will of the Emperor.

It was typical of Lorgar that he had turned humiliation into triumph. No tawdry wiping away of the Legion's history. No amendments to the records of Terra away from scrutiny. Here, where he had first claimed a world for the Emperor, he ordered his Legion to make public amends for their trespasses. As visible and as grand as had been the trespasses against the Emperor, so too would be the penance to atone for them.

With them the Word Bearers had brought the sum of their wisdom and faith: every book and scrap of plex, crystal or parchment containing invocation and prayer; every banner, icon and aquila; every purity seal and oathpaper; every reliquary and talisman.

Lorgar said nothing. All knew why they were there.

He started the first pyre, throwing a votive candle onto an oil-soaked heap of prayer mats emblazoned with the Colchisian rune of the One – whose 'I' shape outsiders mistook as shorthand for Imperium – variously rendered with additional bars, wings, skulls or haloes.

Of all the blazes Kor Phaeron had witnessed of late, this was the crowning moment. On the face of things, seen through the eyes of most there still, and in the reports of the Legio Custodes that would be sent back to Terra, it was a highly visible purge of the Legion's Emperor-worship.

And, in truth, it was.

Yet what few knew and no others saw, was that worship of another kind would replace it. Already through the Brotherhood Kor Phaeron had placed Chaplains and captains educated in the ways of the 'Old Faith'. The Truth, the people of Colchis had called it. The Lore and the Law of the Powers. There were still enough of that world and generation to remember what had come before to spread the Word to later generations.

Had he known what would come to pass... Kor Phaeron corrected himself. He had known, though the specifics he would not have dared guess at. But always he had attested to the plans of the Powers and how they acted through him. They had led him to Lorgar and from that moment destined him to this fiery apotheosis of his faith.

A whole Legion of Space Marines dedicated to the prosecution of the Powers' goals, nestled in the heart of the Imperium's efforts to conquer the galaxy.

He caught Erebus looking at him, skull helm held in his hands. There was triumph there too and Kor Phaeron realised he was smiling. He assumed a more respectful expression, yet returned the look of the First Chaplain in acknowledgement of the moment and their achievement.

His eye was drawn to Lorgar. He thought perhaps he might see some recognition there also, but the Urizen's eyes were lifted aloft, staring up into the Empyrean beyond the vaults of the massive temple. Around him the Word Bearers approached, hurling their banners and books, scrolls and sacraments onto the growing fire.

The primarch's eyes were ablaze with a golden light, a look Kor Phaeron knew well. The Golden One was not seeing anything in the physical realm, nor paying heed to the mortals who passed him, or the lick of the flames creeping closer and closer. The music of the spheres moved him, that higher calling, the universe's symphony that only came to his ear.

His purpose, his perception of the galaxy unlike any other.

Uncertainty crept into Kor Phaeron's heart at this thought.

Had the Powers guided him to the Declined on that day to meet the vehicle of his elevation? Or... Was it possible that they had guided Lorgar to a nearby caravan, which happened to belong to an itinerant, disgraced preacher?

Like the slow dusk of Colchis, a chill spread through Kor Phaeron despite the increasing fury of the temple-pyre.

All have their place in the scheme of the Powers. He had assumed that his zeal had been rewarded, the delivery of Lorgar the means by which Kor Phaeron would bring about their pre-eminence. It seemed prideful, now that he considered it.

Yet it had been his hand that had steered events. It had been the endeavours and machinations of Kor Phaeron that had... that had delivered Lorgar to Vharadesh, the heart of the Covenant. Where he almost certainly would have ended up by any other route. Such was the nature of the Covenant it was inevitable that Lorgar would have joined their ranks.

Kor Phaeron's confidence rallied briefly as he considered his part in creating the myth of Lorgar that had seen the Covenant capitulate without a fight. The resurgence fluttered away like the scraps of parchment being carried on the thermals of the flames. Lorgar's primarch gifts would have seen him dominate the Church of Colchis under any circumstance, whether physical or moral.

In fact, Kor Phaeron's exile and tutelage had delayed that ascension by several years.

It was folly to doubt, he chided himself. Where was the strength he had shown in moulding Lorgar into the leader he was today? The teacher and acolyte. Yes, that was all Kor Phaeron's doing. Perhaps it was a little arrogant to think he deserved all of the credit, but he had guided Lorgar well and the primarch had recognised that, rewarded his contribution and loyalty.

Tutor and student.

Father and son.

Indivisible.

He sought the gaze of the Golden One to reassure himself, to see something of their bond renewed in the Urizen's eyes. Still there was nothing, only the faraway look of a man occupying a different realm.

If Kor Phaeron stepped aside, there would be... a literal legion of willing devotees to do the bidding of their primarch. Kor Phaeron was despised by most, his position despite not being a Space Marine a spark that lit the jealousy of many in the XVII.

His manner with inferiors had gained him few allies, even among the Brotherhood. That clandestine sect was built upon secrecy and a complete lack of compassion. But they answered to the Keeper of Faith; they would never turn on him.

It was a delusion, quickly stripped bare by Kor Phaeron's new-found enlightenment. Lorgar commanded the Brotherhood, and at his word they would rid the universe of Kor Phaeron as easily as they had the Terrans and the Colchisians too enraptured by the worship of the Emperor to accept the new order, their Old Faith.

More and more of the Legion's panoply was piled onto the burning mounds. All of it sacrificed, the achievements of the Great Crusade cast aside in a show of contrition.

All a show, Kor Phaeron thought with a lump in his throat and a tightness in his chest.

Lorgar desired a god to worship, above all else, and would stop at nothing to find it. Nothing.

He had endured, for it was the Urizen's way to avoid strife.

Always, despite all setbacks small and grand, Lorgar prevailed. Kor Phaeron thought of the beatings he had given him as a youth. At any moment he might have employed the Voice, could have commanded Kor Phaeron to stop, to obey his merest whim.

But he had not.

Why? Why had he put up with the humiliation, the physical pain, the disdain of his adoptive father?

The surest disguise for his own ambition had been to hide it within the cloak of another's...

All that had occurred, from the moment he had stepped from the tent in the great expanse of Colchis' deserts, Lorgar had desired. Perhaps not desired, but allowed. He had allowed Kor Phaeron to take him from the Declined. He had allowed the chastisement, even speaking and fighting on behalf of his abuser.

And now that he had finally cast off the illusory faith in the Emperor and rededicated himself to the Powers, what now? Did he need Kor Phaeron?

An ember fluttered from the pyre and landed on Kor Phaeron's gauntlet. He brushed it away, turning it to ashen dust.

Lorgar would dispose of him as easily as he sloughed away all previous faiths and guises. Always with regret, always with a tear and self-flagellation, but all the same Lorgar removed every obstacle between himself and his goal.

Staring ahead, lost in the flames, Kor Phaeron wondered when he too would be thrown upon a pyre, just another obstacle between Lorgar and immortal greatness.

ABOUT THE AUTHOR

Gav Thorpe is the author of the Horus Heresy novels *Deliverance Lost, Angels of Caliban* and *Corax,* as well as the novella *The Lion,* which formed part of the *New York Times* bestselling collection *The Primarchs*. He is particularly well-known for his Dark Angels stories, including the *Legacy of Caliban* series. His Warhammer 40,000 repertoire further includes the *Path of the Eldar* series, the Phoenix Lords novels *Jain Zar* and *Asurmen,* The Beast Arises novels *The Emperor Expects* and *The Beast Must Die,* Horus Heresy audio dramas *The Thirteenth Wolf, Raven's Flight, Honour to the Dead* and *Raptor,* and a multiplicity of short stories. For Warhammer, Gav has penned the End Times novel *The Curse of Khaine,* the Time of Legends trilogy, *The Sundering,* and much more besides. He lives and works in Nottingham.

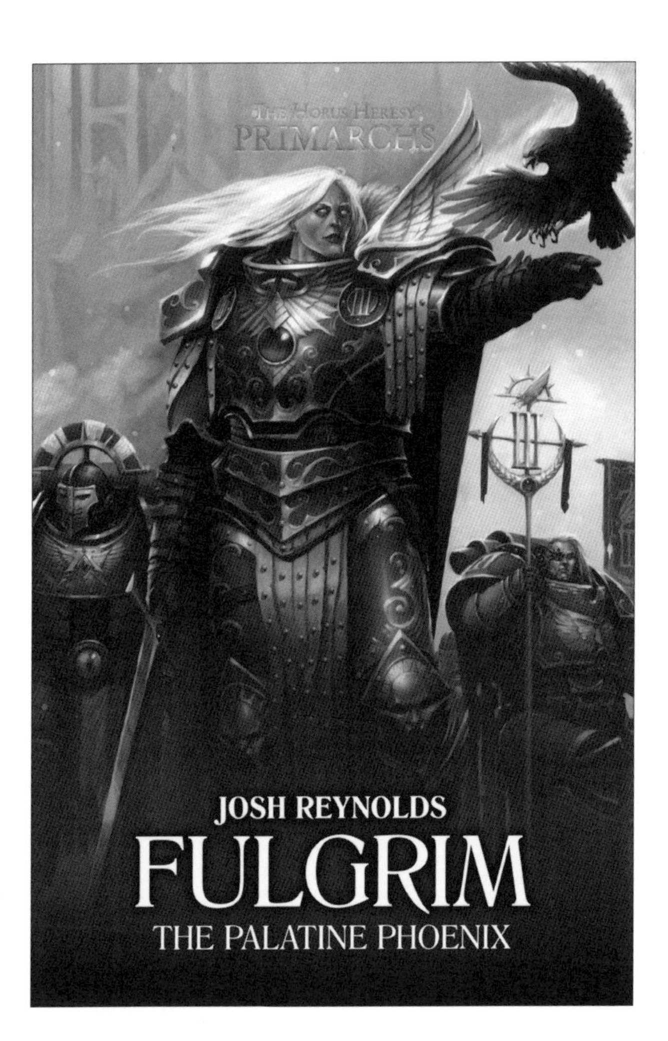
THE HORUS HERESY
PRIMARCHS
JOSH REYNOLDS
FULGRIM
THE PALATINE PHOENIX

An extract from

FULGRIM

THE PALATINE PHOENIX

by Josh Reynolds

Fire and blood.

It always came down to fire and blood. Or so his brothers, in their wisdom, claimed. Compliance was forged in fire and cooled in blood, they said. Skies of ash and fields of bone. Fire and blood. A monotonous philosophy, lacking in even the crudest artistry.

It frustrated him to no end that such a belief was the guiding star of humanity's great adventure. Even the Emperor seemed to hold to it, though more for efficiency's sake than any other reason. Fire and blood. Efficiency and speed. The watchwords of the Great Crusade.

'Efficiency,' Fulgrim said, making it sound like a prayer. The Phoenician stared out through the glass of the viewport, idly calculating the distances between the stars that glimmered in the black. The observation bay of the *Pride of the Emperor* was dimly lit and stripped bare of all decoration. Here, there was nothing to distract one from the immensity of the universe, and the grandeur of the stars that populated it.

The primarch of the Emperor's Children was clad only in simple robes of white and purple, a mantle of feathers and gold draped over his deceptively broad shoulders. Armour was for war, or parades. Here, in his place of contemplation, he wore what he considered appropriately subdued attire. It fit loose about his lean form and added to the regal serenity of his appearance. His sole concession to practicality was the blade belted low on his waist. One hand rested on its pommel, and a finger traced the wires wrapped tight about the hilt.

A gift, that blade. A sign of love, forged in respect. He treasured it above all else, save his own certainty. The blade and what it meant were signs that he was on the right path. That he had not turned his back on destiny, but rather embraced it.

He studied the reflections of the amethyst-armoured legionaries of the Third who stood at attention behind him. Clad in thunderbolt and rayed sun, the palatine aquila displayed prominently, they seemed as the demigods of myth made flesh and bound in ceramite. He stood head and shoulders above the tallest of them, a god among demigods, his white hair tied in a single, serpentine braid. Violet eyes, set into pale features that were honed to sharp perfection, narrowed in contemplation.

The six Space Marines arrayed behind him were among the best and the brightest of the current crop. Only one of the six was of the Two Hundred – the original remnants of the Legion who'd knelt before him on Chemos. A seventh, also a member of the Two Hundred, stood somewhat apart and behind the others, watching in silence. He nodded slightly, as if aware of Fulgrim's observation. Fulgrim stifled a snort of amusement.

Five of the six were eager young warriors, freshly blooded and bursting with the need to prove themselves. Much like himself. He pushed the thought aside, annoyed at the sting of truth. He focused on the others, noting their nervousness. To a human, they might seem as statues, barely moving or giving any sign of emotion. But to him, their inner turmoil was plain to see. The five did not know why they had been called into his presence, and it made them nervous. The sixth seemed to feel nothing at all. He smiled, despite this.

'What is the definition of efficiency, Narvo?' he asked, gesturing to one without turning around. A bit of showmanship never hurt.

Legionary Narvo Quin stiffened, obviously surprised to be singled out by his primarch. 'Victory through minimal effort, my lord.' Quin was a hammer amongst blades. A brawler by nature. But the occasional flash of insight implied potential. A common thread amongst them. Their potential was obvious. And this was all about potential.

Fulgrim turned from his calculations of the stars and their distances, holding the numbers fixed in his head. 'An acceptable answer, if somewhat pedestrian.' Quin shifted his weight, chagrin evident in his posture. Fulgrim continued. 'In truth, efficiency requires more effort than the minimal. And what is or is not efficient can only be properly determined through context. A lesson I learned as a child, amongst ore processors and mineral scoops.'

Without looking, he reached out and tapped the glass with a pale finger. Slowly, carefully, he drew a continuous line between the stars. 'What Horus considers adequate, for instance, others might call grossly barbaric.' For several decades, his dwindled Legion had fought in the shadow of another. Horus had shown him what it meant to be one of the Emperor's sons, with all the duties and responsibilities that entailed. A flash of perfect teeth, as he recalled the frustrations of those days. 'Then, the efficiency of wolves is a thing unto itself, and not to be judged by the likes of us.'

He turned back to the stars as a polite chuckle rippled through the group. 'However, we can judge our own efficiency, or lack thereof.' The chuckles ceased, as he'd intended. There was a time and a place for humour. He knocked on the glass of the viewport with a bare knuckle. 'My brothers leave behind them a trail of worlds broken to the wheel. Scars of fire and blood, carved across the face of the galaxy. I think – I know – that there is a better way.'

Another smile, swift and sure like the slash of a blade. 'A more efficient way. And together, you and I will prove it.'

He traced a circle around one particular point of light. 'This is Twenty-Eight One. Byzas, to its inhabitants, of whom there are several billion. A not inconsiderable number, given what it has endured of late.' He looked at his warriors. 'We will bring Byzas into compliance. But not through fire and blood. Six blades and six blades alone will I carry into this battle. You are those blades.'

Their faces were rife with emotion. Not just pride, but worry and eagerness and calculation. They were young. Blooded but untested. This would be their test, and his as well. A new method of war, perfect in its conception and practice.

'This is the first step on a new journey, the beginning of a new war. One we will win, with our own hands and our own strength. This is the first chapter of our story. All else has been but prologue.' He tapped the mote of Byzas. 'There is a term in the Augean dialect of the Ionic Plateau – anabasis. The journey an army takes inland from the sea. The march upcountry to new conquests.' He turned, arms spread, like a king of old anointing his knights. 'This, my sons, is our anabasis.'

As one, they knelt, fists clenched tight against the palatine aquila that marked their armour.

Fulgrim smiled, pleased. 'I have chosen you six to represent the whole of our Legion. You will be my equerries in this matter. Think on what that means, and prepare yourselves accordingly.' He turned back to the viewport.

'Go. You are dismissed.'

The legionaries departed, talking quietly among themselves. Two more quietly than others. One said nothing at all. When they had gone, Fulgrim said, 'You may speak freely now, Abdemon.'

He turned to face the seventh of those he'd summoned. Clad in Tyrian-laquered battleplate, Lord Commander Abdemon was a walking example of all that the warriors of the Legion should aspire to be. His hand rested on the pommel-stone of the artificer-wrought power sword sheathed at his waist. The delicate looking sabre had been a gift from the armourers of the Ionic Plateau on Terra. Abdemon was reportedly a swordsman of some skill, though Fulgrim had, as yet, not witnessed it for himself. At the moment, it wasn't his ability with a blade that Fulgrim required of him.

The lord commander was one of his senior officers, and a respected voice in his councils. Abdemon was respectful, without succumbing to sycophancy. Of the ten commanders of the first ten millennials of the Legion, he was perhaps the most thoughtful. It was that inclination to consideration that Fulgrim needed now.

'What did you think?' Fulgrim asked.

'Very stirring, my lord,' Abdemon said. His voice was a soft rasp, like steel sliding through silk. 'I felt my heart quicken to hear it.'

Fulgrim quirked an eyebrow. 'Oh? You didn't think it was a bit much?'

'No, my lord. Just the right amount of jingoism.' Abdemon was Terran. He had been among those who made that first, fateful journey to Chemos with the Emperor, and knelt at Fulgrim's feet. He had fought at the forefront of every battle the Third Legion had participated in, including Proxima. He had earned rank and respect in equal measure, and Fulgrim had swiftly deduced that winning him over was the key to winning the Legion.

That he was their gene-father had been no surety of loyalty, or love. Sons turned against fathers every day, on a thousand worlds. And the fracturing of the Legion had weakened the command structure to a concerning degree. They were used to fighting as individuals, or as small groups, rather than a Legion. It had taken long years on his part, and that of his trusted lord commanders, to rebuild their sense of purpose and their discipline.

Fulgrim snorted at Abdemon's words. 'You'd best thank whatever star you were born under that I have a sense of humour, Abdemon. Otherwise, I'd have you punished for such blatant disrespect.'

Abdemon bowed his head. White hair, bound in short, thick braids, was pulled back from his dark face in a tight bundle, giving him a hawk-like aspect. Fulgrim fancied there was something of him in Abdemon's aspect, though the officer would never be handsome. He doubted Abdemon cared.

'My apologies, my lord. I shall endeavour to curtail such foolishness in the future.' Fulgrim heard the smile in the words, though Abdemon's face was as still as the onyx it seemed to have been carved from.

'And now you compound your insolence with bald-faced lies,' Fulgrim said. He laid the edge of his hand against the side of Abdemon's neck. Gently, only gently, but in warning all the same. He felt Abdemon's pulse jump, in sudden disquiet. Not fear though, which pleased him. His sons – the true sons of the Emperor – were above fear.

Fulgrim leaned low, so that Abdemon would feel the full effect of his voice. The lord commander's pulse quickened. It was no easy thing for a Space Marine to be in close proximity to their primarch. Abdemon handled it better than most, but even he was affected by it. 'Carefully now, and only in private, or I'll be forced to make an example of you. The chain of command must be seen to be maintained, Abdemon.'

Abdemon didn't meet his gaze. 'As you command.' A Space Marine couldn't be seen to disrespect his primarch, even in jest. Especially important for the Third, as their numbers were as yet still so few, and their morale only just recovered from the depths to which it had plunged in the years before Fulgrim had taken his place at their head.